HARLIE HARGRAVES

The Mush

a horror novel

To Molly from The Found Us.
You are a survivor that I envy.

Also, FUCK CANCER!

Contents

Content Warning!

This is a horror novel. It's meant to freak readers out and make them question things. I'm a very nice person despite the dark content I write. So, to show how nice I am, here is the list of everything that is in this book. The content warnings include:

- Suicide/death of a parent (On-page, Prologue)
- Bodily gore
- Death of a beloved pet (On-page)
- Homophobia
- Final act 'get together' of love interests
- Murder (On and off-page)
- Explicit language
- Acts of violence
- Talk/mention of alcohol abuse (On and off-page)
- Some super gross shit…
- Talk/mention of cancer
- Physical/emotional abuse

There might be more warnings that I missed. My bad. Anyway, happy reading!

PS. If any of these content warnings make you uncomfortable

I highly advise you not to read this book. Your mental health is too important to be ruined by my disgusting work of art…

Prologue

The stout stench of Jack Daniels whiskey permeates the air of Mom and Dad's bedroom. There's a collection of glass bottles on her side of the room. I think they're her favorite since they never seem to stop showing up. I wonder if it tastes the way it looks. Sweet like fizzy apple juice.

It's a sour smell that singes the inside of my nose as I continue to hide in their closet surrounded by thick winter coats and canvas rain jackets. This is my special place to get away from her sickness called alcoholism. At least that's what Dad called it when he tried explaining her outbursts to me.

I'm still not sure what it means but I haven't dared to bring up the subject again. If Mom hears the word 'alcoholic' uttered then she'll go ballistic and perhaps break the front door again. That's only when my dad whispered it under his breath that one time two months about before school started.

I've grown disgusted with the potent scent that hangs on her tongue from her favorite drinks and the loudness she brings home from the bar. I struggle to hold a gag in each time she places a wet kiss upon my overly plump cheek.

She loves the old saloon down the road. It's a place where

1

the broken and lonely go to fill the void that lingers in their hearts. I think it's rather sad. Like a sad episode of *Full House* that plays on reruns in the middle of the night from the big TV that used to be in the living room.

My mom broke that too.

This time Dad decided to wait for her in the living room. He knew she would be coming home in a fit when the clock struck ten. She never came home after she got off at her top-secret job that they never talked to me about. Maybe it's a good thing I don't understand why he makes her leave her work clothes out on the back porch.

It's weird when she hobbles upstairs in just her pointy bra and undies shouting about random things that never make sense to me.

Once her car pulled into the driveway at a fast speed Dad forced me up the stairs and into my room. Of course, I didn't stay there for long. But when she stumbled inside our two-story house her high voice filled the living room. I expected them to stay down there when the arguing started.

Dad following Mom up the stairs to their room after I just barely managed to get in the closet was surely a surprise. My heart stalled its beats for longer than I expected.

"You smell horrible. How much did you drink this time, Honey?" Dad tries to use a calm voice. It never really soothes her like it used to. I like to hear it during story time when Dad tucks me into bed.

Her huff is an indication that she won't be tolerating his reasonable tone tonight. She should be grateful for him. Most of the time I don't find her worthy of his kindness. She can be meaner than the bullies at school who make fun of my continuous scrunchy face. I can't help the way my nose

2

crinkles with every expression I make.

I peek out of the cracked door. Mom is ruffling her thick curly red hair. It shines like a thousand pennies in the light from the lamp that sits on the bedside table.

"Oh, like you're so damn innocent. Can't I have a few drinks after a bad day at work?" Mom wrinkles her button nose, a feature that I share with her. The freckles covering her nose, those I wish I had. So pretty like cinnamon powder on pumpkin pie.

"No, that's not what I'm saying." Dad shakes his head at her stern attitude. He always does his best not to fight back. Her words might wound his heart but he is a brave man. I admire that about him. He can stand up to the boogie man himself if he wants.

Mom rips off her long green cardigan before tossing it towards me and the closet. I rush to clamp my mouth shut with my hands as it collides with a wicked force. They can't know that I'm in here watching this.

"Damn you, Brian!" Her earsplitting shriek causes me to cringe. I rush to grab a random sweater that rots at the bottom of the closet, clutching it to my chest, wishing Dad could hold me and tell me a story.

He rubs his face roughly. Those tired green eyes, like mine, are rimmed with unshed tears. "We don't need to do this. Put the suitcase down. Let's talk downstairs so Charlie won't hear us."

I watch Mom take the light brown suitcase that's been sitting at the foot of their bed for weeks. She's been threatening to leave him when I'm not around. They think I'm never there when they have these heated talks. Truth be told, I have a really bad habit of spying on them. At first, I thought their

3

little spats were funny. But then they got worse. Then I just never stopped listening to them out of fear of one day missing something big. Something like this.

My chest aches from watching Mom toss her things into the suitcase. Dad attempts to pull her away. She hits him hard across the face. The slap echoes into the now silent house.

Tears of fear drip down my face. I use my short curly hair to stifle my cries. Why don't they ever get along? It hurts to see them like this.

"I am so sick of you telling me what to do. I'm sick of you!" Mom shouts at Dad, the only person who hasn't given up on her. I have. I did a long time ago when I learned what fancy drinks were and what they do to the ones you love.

Dad backs up a few steps towards the door. Streaks of nervous sweat trickle down his face as Mom aims his shotgun at him. He keeps it under the bed in case of emergencies. What is she going to do with it? As I take a moment to think, it hits me hard.

Oh, Dad.

My heart squeezes from something I can't describe. I don't want to watch anymore. Maybe if they both turn around I can sneak back to my room. Yes, that's a good plan.

"Honey, put the gun down. We can talk this through. We always do."

"I want to end this."

"End what?"

"Us!" Mom belts in agony.

I can't tell if she's hurt or not. Somehow my teeth have found my bottom lip. I have been biting down so hard that my lip has split and now warm blood trails down my chin. In a quick motion, I wipe it off with the sweater I'm holding.

4

Dad smiles at her the best he can despite his lips twitching from terror. The ticking watch on his left wrist glints in the light shining into the room from the hall. The glare of it temporarily blinds me as he raises his arms in surrender.

I don't see Mom take her first shot. The shotgun screams when the bullet leaves the large barrel chamber. When I regain my sight I peer out of the closet door. Dad is on his knees, gripping his left shoulder as ripples of blood flow between his shaking fingers.

A silent gasp escapes me when I see Mom aim the gun underneath her chin. Dad notices this too and rushes to his feet, a slight stagger filling his moments.

"Baby? My sweet wife? Please, put it down. We'll get you some help."

At this moment, I know no matter how hard you try to help those who can't seem to find the courage to help themselves, they will choose the path of darkness.

"No!"

"Mommy!"

Dad doesn't get the gun from Mom in time. The final shot rings in my ears as I fly out of the closet. Just like him, I'm too late.

A thick splatter of brain matter and blood clings to us. I feel it on my face. Without warning, vomit shoots up my esophagus and out of my mouth. And just as quickly as it came my sudden sickness was gone. That's when my mouth drops open and I scream.

I screamed because I just watched my mother kill herself. A moment I never thought would be possible.

I screamed due to the fact my dad will now forever blame himself for not helping her in time. Observing the way he brings her limp body into his lap is enough for me to sob.

I screamed to the high heavens in anger, hoping someone or something would hear and tell me they could make it better. Why? Why did this have to happen to us?

And despite me being so damn young to understand really anything I knew this would forever haunt me and my dreams.

Act I

THE DEATH

1. Butter Popcorn & Green Goop

I must have been abducted by little green aliens last night and dumped onto Planet Freak. The coarse paper movie ticket I'm clenching for dear life in my fingers was not supposed to be six fucking dollars. Last year every movie ticket was four bucks or less.

Yep, I've been kidnapped and woken up in an alternate universe. Just my fucking luck!

"Can you take a chill pill? That vein in your forehead is going to pop if you keep doing that." Crista Fisher, a short girl with long fire hair who loves to wear funky chunky sweaters, even in the middle of summer, tries to soothe out the crease in between my brows. Her fingers are cool against my heated skin.

She's telling me to chill? She mustn't since her thick pin-straight hair is almost all plastered to her sweaty cheeks. Maybe she should have done more than put half of it in a ponytail. And I'm sure her cute wispy bangs don't help.

With a deep huff, I swat her hand away from my face. She jerks back into the chest of her tall boyfriend. Thomas Jones, a literal beanstalk, grips Crista's shoulders with a grin plastered on his plump rose lips. His shaggy black curls fall over his stormy blue eyes, making him the total badass. The leather jacket he always wears does the job of pulling his bad-boy look together.

No wonder Crista is hooked on him like a child with candy. I would be too if that kind of guy was my type.

"I wouldn't wake the beast if I were you, Love Bug." He brings his mouth to her neck and plants many irritating loud kisses to her skin. I visibly cringe.

She squeals like a pig and accidentally bumps into me. I shove her off with a playful smirk of my own, all my sudden agitation now disappearing due to their silliness.

All three of us quickly sober up as we walk through the doors of the newly renovated movie theater. My jaw drops in awe after noticing bright new spotlights shining down in the main hall where people get their snacks and drinks.

Now this was worth waiting all school year for. Gosh, I never want to wait that long again to see a new film.

9

"Wow, this is awesome." Crista smiles wide as she takes in the sight of the fresh red velvet carpet that leads to various registers and concession stands. It matches well with the dark red walls too. Her large doe eyes the color of molten honey glow in wonder. The rays of yellow light make her pale skin appear two shades darker. I'm not sure how that's possible.

I do know that this place has really outdone itself. The new fancy red ropes guarding the entrance to each movie room are adorned with gold tassels at each end. Where did they get the budget for those?

"Wow, indeed." I echo her words from earlier when I let my eyes race around the massive room. Groups of all kinds of people gather at every booth. Young children tug on their mother's shirt, begging for an ice cream cone. Elderly couples ask the theater works many questions about what's in the nacho cheese and why the popcorn is cheaper than their pickles. Now that is familiar.

I bite the inside of my cheek to keep from smiling at the familiar rustling of voices and the smell of melted butter and popcorn salt.

"Oh, hey!" Crista beams at the person who steps directly in my path, blocking me from the nearest concession booth.

My breath hangs tight in the back of my throat. A nervous sweat hurries to cling to my palms. The corners of my lips twitch at the abrupt sight of Bucky Sinclair, my best friend and love of my life. But, he doesn't know about that last part.

His much larger frame casts a shadow over the three of us.

"Hey. What's good?" He partakes in a manly handshake with Thomas. They collide roughly, patting each other on the back as if they hadn't just seen each other yesterday evening.

Ugh, boys.

Once their greeting turns into a heated conversation about cars I take this moment to really look at him. His loose dark curls with crisp blonde highlights truly frame his sharp face perfectly. The overhead lighting doesn't do his light brown skin any justice or his hazel eyes. The green in them just sticks out like a spotlight.

God, why did you make him so damn handsome? He's so enticing. I think I might drool. What am I thinking? I've got to pull my shit together and be the cool badass chick that I am.

When his eyes drift over to us I rush to straighten my back and force a stern expression on my face.

He and Thomas approach me and Crista who has been clinging to my arm the moment her lover left her embrace. She always needs to have a hold of someone. I'm not one for physical contact, but for her, I'll do anything. I guess it's a girl thing.

"I see you guys got here an hour early. The movie doesn't start till what? Nine?" Bucky makes a show of checking an invisible watch on his left wrist that's a part of his muscular throwing arm for football. The sleeve of his purple and green letterman jacket scrunch with his fluid movements.

I scoff. "Does it matter when it starts? I want us to get the highest seats. Do you have a problem with that, Bucky?"

His wide smile that shows off his pearl-white teeth always throws me off. My stomach does a flip.

"Nope. Not at all." He confesses and then glides forward to rope me in his too-warm hug. I take this as a sign to finally laugh with the others. I hate to admit him touching me feels good even with his armpit catching my long curly blonde hair. I fight the urge to tug away.

This moment is too good to ruin.

11

"C'mon! I need popcorn." Crista's playful huff kicks Thomas into gear. He takes her hands and gives her a sickening kiss before tugging her away from us. Her joyous laughter has me grinning like an idiot. I love these guys. Well, love for Bucky is a strong word. I like him very much. Actually, I love him like a friend.

Who am I trying to convince that I'm not totally into him? No one but myself.

"Hey, whatcha thinking about in that big mind of yours?" It's his deep voice that yanks me out of my frazzled mind.

I shake my head as he guides us over to follow after our friends. Without thinking, I weave my fingers with his. He and I both freeze slightly. Neither of us acknowledge what I just did. That is certainly for the best.

When Crista looks over her shoulder covered in an extra fuzzy yellow cardigan I tear myself out of Bucky's hold to join her. I miss the heat his body pushed onto me. I crave his scent which is football leather and cheap cologne.

However, I shake off the empty feeling in my gut. It's easy to do once I get a sight of the many delicious treats that are kept in the glass case beneath the register. Studying all the sour gummies and tart cakes wrapped in clear decorative paper makes my mouth water.

Thomas retrieves his worn black leather wallet that matches his jacket out of his back jean pocket. He pulls it open with an arched brow. I bite the inside of my cheek to hold in a chuckle. His expressions kill me.

"So, what will it be, Shocker Pictures?" The sound of our independent film production company name causes my heart to flutter.

With a dramatic sigh, I point down to the can of Cheez Balls.

Crista giggles before gesturing to a pack of Big League Chew. She comes to the movies every weekend and chooses gum to snack on. What a weirdo.

Thomas peers at the four of our strange crew. "And you, Mister Football Man?"

Bucky offers a gentle smile. "I'll take the same as Charlie."

The one who seems to be calling all the financial shots nods his head before reporting back to the cashier chick. I ignore the feeling of Bucky's heat-filled eyes on me.

I want to sigh in relief after realizing that I'm not the only one dressed up to see *A Nightmare On Elm Street 4.* For months since its first trailer, I've been saving up money for art supplies to build my own custom sweater shirt. A few other people in the hall have theirs on, but none look as authentic as mine. I took charge and made plenty of screen-accurate rips. Even with those the green and red stripes weren't enough. It wasn't a big decision to sneak away Dad's lighter to crisp a few of the rips. He needs to stop smoking anyway.

After tinkering around and pulling a few strings the sweater finally looked like Freddy's.

I am the most awesome person I know. Well, there are my friends who are also kind of awesome. But I'm not going to tell them that. Their egos might orgasm at the little praise that confession offers.

Thomas pays for our treats like a proud grownup. Crista, the mother of our odd group, hands them to us. I grip my blue can tightly before marching ahead.

Despite my height and soft green eyes, I am this crew's unofficial leader. None of them object to it because they know I have their backs through anything. Even if that means hiding a few of their skeletons in my closet.

And I have a very big and disturbing closet.

My mouth hangs open as the gruesome yet beautiful images dance across the movie screen.

Cries and screams from Freddy's victims influence my mind to form moving pictures of my own. The way the set had been created to somehow empower the villain ends up working in the main heroine's favor. I find it most useful when thinking up my own set for our ongoing film. It's about a wannabe theater chick who wants to make it big in New York. Of course, it won't be that easy when she's stalked by a wicked werewolf.

The film was my idea. And it is a very clever one if I do say so myself.

"This is actually horrendous." Crista fakes a gag and stuffs her face into the leather of Thomas's sleeve.

"Awe, my poor Love Bug." He coos to her as a particularly gory scene breaks into one of great terror before our eyes.

It's easy to ignore their whines. My body leans forward, letting me sit on the very edge of my seat. My gaze inhales the many bright colors that somehow work with the much darker ones. This fantasy world is one that I want to jump into and never come back out of. Maybe if I dream when going to bed tonight I'll be sucked into a land much like this one. There I can take note of what makes it all tick, how people think in such ways.

I hear Bucky fiddle with the small camera that I let him hold as we sat down in our seats almost an hour ago.

Over the years of hanging out with him, I've noticed he likes to mess with things with his fingers. It either keeps him calm or clears his head of unwanted thoughts. In most cases, he messes around with my fingers.

But tonight I'm too preoccupied with the movie in front of me.

He knows this or else he would have taken my hand in his a long time ago.

However, my brewing mind is most rudely interrupted by loud coughing. It's at the very front of the movie screen. Whoever it is seems to not be having the best time.

Sucks for them.

I figure they will drink a sip of their soda or bottled water and be right again. But boy am I wrong.

The rough coughing continues. It sounds wet and hurtful.

"Hey, can you shut up?" A voice calls out which happens to be louder than the person's hacking.

"Dude, you're ruining the movie!" Another person shouts in distress.

More and more people get loud. Soon the entire theater room erupts in annoyed groans and harsh snarls.

The lights flicker back on and the new movie is now paused.

I sit back in the seat with a huff. "Damn."

The coughs turn violent. The person rises from their seat

15

looking horrible. It's Amy Driscal. Oh, holy shit does she look awful.

Everyone seems to notice her sweaty skin that is tinged green and the gruesome open wounds that litter her skin. Who let her in like this? Is she okay?

Curiosity fuels my movements. I'm up on my feet, my hands now urging for Bucky to give me the camera. It's moments like that that deserve to be filmed. I flip over the viewer and shove it into Thomas's hand.

"Get some good angles," I tell him as I move past a worried Bucky. He tries to get a grip of my sweater but I'm already on the steps that lead down to the doors.

I won't stay still when something new and exciting is brewing right before my eyes.

"I-I don't feel so good." Amy's words are muddled. Big glops of dark green goop leak from her mouth. Another cough makes its way out of her. She chokes on her oddly colored vomit, accidentally spraying some of it onto the row behind her. I watch a few chunks land on their faces. A few of them bend forward to puke before their seats. I gulp down my own bile.

Cries of disgust fill the air. Many people get up to leave. I only get closer to the scene. Now either due to curiosity or concern for Amy. I guess it doesn't matter which.

Before I can even approach her hefty arms dip around my waist to yank me back into a rock-solid chest.

"No, I need to ask her questions!" I try clawing at Bucky's arms but it's no use.

We're halfway out of the movie room when cops and paramedics rush past us.

He roughly shakes me before placing me back on my feet.

16

During my agitated need for answers about what the fuck was going on I didn't notice we were already out of the building.

I toss my brown Freddy hat to the pavement and growl. "C'mon, that was a great shot!"

Crista shivers in disgust. "I don't even want to know what that was."

"Well, I got something with the camera. The dim lights didn't give us much to work with though." Thomas shakes his head as he plays back the footage.

Bucky attempts to touch my shoulders. I move out of the way to look at the video before he can get a hold of me. I will regret that later.

Watching what Thomas filmed is strange. Amy was sweating like crazy and her poor skin was littered with open lesions that leaked a nasty green sludge. And the green goop she was choking on is disgusting. Now I feel horrible for wanting to catch some sort of story. I'm not no damn news reporter.

Why did I act like that? *Because you crave chaos, you freak.*

I step away and shake my head free of the image. Whatever was going on with her will be fixed. She will be better and return to her City Hall secretary position she's been wanting our entire high school career. It's going to be alright.

I jolt when new footsteps make their way out of the theater building.

It's Sheriff Osburn and Deputy Crain. He doesn't look too happy with his thick gray mustache twitching.

He places his hands on his hips in a firm motion. I gulp down the nerves that do their best to rupture my stomach. I'm glad that Thomas knows to hide the camera behind his back. No need for the sheriff to take what's mine when we technically did nothing wrong.

"I need y'all to go home." Sheriff Osburn twists his head. That shrill voice of his makes my eardrums itch.

All four of us nod our heads, turn around swiftly, and sprint to the '67 Chevy Impala that's parked at the far side of the parking lot.

A wicked smile graces my lips as I retrieve the keys from my pocket and unlock the epic car.

"Go, go!" Thomas shouts a joyous tune when slapping the headrest of my seat. I shift the car gear into drive and spin out of the parking lot with rock music blasting in our ears.

It's a rather addicting thrill to almost be caught in the wrong. It's an even better feeling to have others at your side during the awesome ride.

I drop off each of my friends at their house. Crista seems fine. She just needs a good rest. Thomas is just as perky as ever. He howls before strutting onto his porch. Now, Bucky is something else. He says nothing to me as he gets out of the car. His eyes, however, say all that he wants to say to me. At least I like to think so.

The soft brown orbs freckled with specks of chilling green seem to say 'be careful' and 'I'll call you in a bit'.

With a gentle nod, I speed down his street and to my house. There I find my lovely German Shepherd Copper waiting for me in the driveway. The sight of his amber eyes is enough to make me smile big.

Ah, it's good to be home after watching yet another gory movie that has all the best vibes. I want to make a movie just like that someday.

2. Cruising Through Elora Falls, Oregon

E arly morning sunshine seeps through the frilly pink curtains of the French windows of my room. The light fractures onto the green-painted wallpaper that has floral gold foiling, hitting my eyes at the right angle and ruining my chances of oversleeping.

Once I'm sure that it's not going away any time soon I groan loudly into my pillow, stuffing my face into its soft pale blue covering. It's a soothing sensation on my skin that offers a moment of comfort before I force myself into an upright position.

My eyes sting from the strong yellow rays. I should have closed the curtain before I passed out last night. It would have saved me the trouble of being rudely awoken.

I take my time rubbing the sleep from my aching lids. Small pieces of crust that formed around my lashes crumble onto my fingers.

A pang of cringe enters my chest. "Gross."

I hurry to get the overnight gunk off my hands, leaning over the bed to shake my fingers. Once I'm satisfied that nothing remains, I reel back and flop my arms over my pink and blue striped comforter adorned with bright white stars. With a tilt of my head, I closely examine the fabric, letting my fingers drag across the quilt material. It's something my mom got when she found out she was pregnant with me. After Dad told me this I vowed never to get rid of it no matter what she did to herself and him.

In an instant, I shove the memory into a dark dark corner of my mind. I toss the comforter off my legs, allowing the chilly air to snuggle around me. At least Dad had turned the air conditioning system on during the night or else I'd be a puddle of sweat right about now.

After getting on my feet, sinking my toes into the neon pink shaggy carpet I use my finger to tap curiously on my chin.

I take a split moment to consider the silence that meets my ears.

"Too quiet." I aim my thoughts to the lovely furry dog currently sitting on the corner of the bed with his ears perked up.

His amber eyes stare at me intently. Sometimes I swear he can understand me. Well, he does know 'sit' and 'stay' like any other perfectly trained dog. That's what I like about him most. He doesn't give me or Dad any fuss.

Copper quirks his head to the side. A large grin spreads across my lips.

I greedily clap my hands together as I skip over to the large gray boom box that is always sitting on top of my dark wooden dresser that's filled with most of my clothes. I mainly use my closet to store a lot of my replica movie props and various raincoats.

"What should we listen to today?" With a shrug of my shoulders, I flip through the channels. I not-so-gracefully shake my head to somehow adjust the thick curly bangs that cover my forehead. I'm sure they are a mess that I'll have to fix before leaving the house later.

A few songs fill the room but nothing catches my interest right away. However, when "Girls Just Want to Have Fun" by Cyndi Lauper shoots through the speakers I get all giddy. It's a song that represents exactly how I plan to feel during this entire summer. I don't let myself even think about what will happen when the month is over.

"Hell yeah!" I let out a screech of excitement.

Copper jolts up in an excited motion, his tongue hanging over his jaws, watching closely as I twirl around the room in a daze.

My feet manage to jump around various shirts and VHS tapes that are scattered on the floor.

Adrenaline caused by this epic music courses through my being. Each quirky lyric and high tone sinks into my mind, clutching my consciousness tight enough to fuel my happy mood. I will myself to keep dancing until I can no longer catch my breath.

With a hefty exhale, I fall back onto the bed, my arms raised high above my head.

Another song starts after the one I just jammed out to. I don't care to listen. I am on a cloud drifting through the sky at such a slow pace that I'm tempted to fall back asleep. The neckline of my oversized Metallica shirt slips over my shoulder as I sit up on my hands. All glee slips from me in a matter of seconds.

I don't mean to let visions of last night flood my mind, but they quickly take over everything. I feel a frown spread on my face. Damnit, I shouldn't be visualizing those green wounds on her arms and neck. An involuntary shiver trickles through my arms and encourages me to shake.

I let out an annoyed grunt. Copper scoots over the bed and gently nudges my hand with his wet snout.

Whatever happened to Amy was strange and disturbing. Right? I sure as shit can't imagine what could do that to someone. Maybe Dad will know what is going on.

"Alright, I'll get dressed and feed you." The dog pays me no mind when I crawl across the bed to reach the curtains. "Here we go."

I yank them open to let in the light that acts as a comforting embrace. My room is directly pointing towards the forest. The tall green cedar and pine trees greet me with their spiny branches. I take this as a sign of good faith and dress in a random white shirt with short navy blue sleeves. It fits snugly against my generous-sized chest. I'm glad it pairs well with the baggy ripped jeans I picked up off the floor.

I sniff it to make sure it smells clean.

However, I'm missing a signature part of me. My eyes dart around the room and come up empty. Where did I put it? Panic sets into my guts as I rummage around my room with trembling fingers. I never go without it. But, last night I didn't wear it with my costume.

This is just fucking fantastic.

"Hey, Copper? Have you seen my jacket?" I shout in question when I rush into the bathroom connected to my room.

Pale yellow light fills my vision as I flip the switch. A breath of relief escapes me when I manage to spot the bright red jacket made from water-resistant material sitting over the tub's edge. Ease settles in me like lava.

"Found it," I mumble to myself and slither my arms through the sleeves.

It doesn't take long to peer into the mirror and tease out my long hair. The wild blonde curls sit on the middle of my back. They have a habit of frizzing out throughout the day so I use the worst amount of hair spray. It might smell like rancid chemicals but it sure does the best damn job. Once I deem my bangs to be perfect I move on to brushing my teeth, my hips jolting to the music filling my room with each swipe of the toothbrush.

I snap my fingers when exiting the bathroom. Copper gives a good woof before jumping off the bed and trotting to the door. I pick up my denim backpack and sling it over my shoulders.

"Hang on a second." I chuckle at the dog's eagerness to fly through the hall once the door is wide open. The loud echo of his feet meeting the hardwood floor down in the kitchen gives me goosebumps.

I hear Dad greet the dog, his words of happiness only making me skip fast down the brown carpet steps.

23

There I find him scratching the back of Copper's ear with a giant smile on his face. Small wrinkles pull at the corner of his eyes. He looks older than usual with those dark bags under his eyes that never seem to go away these days.

As I approach the final step of the stairs I take a grand leap and land with a thud. The sound of my feet meeting the floor snaps Dad out of his petting fit.

"Hey there, Charlie. Got any plans today?" He doesn't wait for my answer when he pulls me into one of his death-gripping hugs.

"Oh, you know it." I manage to make out with my face squished into his shoulder. His red and blue flannel shirt smells like smoke and cologne. Who is Dad trying to smell nice for?

A few heartwarming seconds go by and then I'm finally free of his loving hold. Dad moves into the kitchen and retrieves a glass jar of fresh orange juice. He likes to squeeze them himself. I think he does it to give himself something he can control. Trauma like what we went through will make a person do strange things.

I hop on a wooden stool next to the island that has a dark marble top. Just as soon as I place my bag on the floor next to me Dad plants a small cup of orange juice before me. I give him a small smile before gulping it all down in one go.

He shakes his head. "Keep drinking like that and you'll end up choking one day."

With a shrug of my shoulders, I glance towards the front door. There I spot my rugged black Converse sitting to the side. I guess I have to lace those on my feet before leaving. I can't just dip without shoes. That would be stupid.

His slight laugh warms my heart. He will soon dress in his

post office uniform and make his way to work once I'm out the door. Better not keep anyone waiting.

Copper yelps as I lean over the kitchen island to gently kiss my dad's cheek.

A giggle laces my tongue. I struggle to put on my shoes while standing up. I find myself sitting on the little patch of carpet surrounding the front door entrance. It's not a large foyer but it does its job.

"Charlie?" Dad utters my name in such a starling tone that I pause, my hand seeming to levitate over the gold door handle.

I see the driveway through the fancy glass. The growing morning sun shines down on both of our cars. Dad saved up eight paychecks to buy me the Impala. I'll forever be grateful for him.

"Yeah?" I twist around only to find him standing near the staircase railing. His hands are clenching the wood rails with dear life. Oh, shit. I think I forgot something important to bring up to him.

"Sheriff Osburn called this morning. He said you and the gang had seen what happened with Amy Driscal. I want you to stay out of it. He said everything is just fine. Alright?" Dad looks me dead in the eyes.

I hate it when he gets serious. But is everything really going to be just fine? I bet no one had said that to Amy. They probably sent her to the hospital in the next town over.

A nod is all I give him as I scratch Copper on the side of his head before sprinting out of the house. The door to my Impala opens with grace. I slide into the seat, put the key in, twist it, and listen to the gorgeous engine erupt into life.

I watch Dad step on the front porch that wraps around most of the house. He sends me a wave as I slowly back out of the driveway that's surrounded by large trees.

I let out an excited shout. Whatever nerves I had about last night quickly disappear as I turn the switch of the radio. More music tickles my eardrums. I want to be consumed by the vibes this drive down Pine Road offers.

We live on the last road on the very outskirts of town. It's rather pleasant to be away from all the noise and busyness. Plus, I get to go over the speed limit without the sheriff's department hot on my tail.

Rolling the windows down to let in the warm breeze is a good idea on my part. As I round a loose corner I can see the rapidly moving river that circles Elora Falls, Oregon. This is a place I've grown to love even with all of its flaws. Those are all the racist homophobic old people and messy chicks who like to start trouble where it isn't needed. Despite that, it's a wonderful place to be.

The love in my heart for Elora Falls only increases as I start to drive down Elora Lane. Now this is where most of the action happens. A lot of families coming from old money live down here. Meaning that all three of my friends occupy this street.

I lucked out.

I'm not mad about it either. Who wants to be surrounded by snobs who think they own the world?

Soon the tall two-story houses bleed into shops filled with hiking supplies. I give a nod to the Blockbuster as I pass it. It's one of Shocker Pictures' favorite hangouts. So many movies to choose from, the ultimate heaven.

Sweet scents coming from various bakeries flood my nose. I inhale deeply as the wind blows my hair behind me.

Eventually, I wind around the oddly clean streets and

approach April Square. This is where most of the town events occur. Whether that be yearly carnivals or important town meetings. We haven't had one in a while. Not since the flood last year. The river became too full from the constant rain that mine and other families along the lines of the town border had to be temporarily relocated. Not the most pleasant Spring Break I've had to endure.

I stop at the light. The post flickers a yellow symbol, letting pedestrians walk across for a few seconds. Once my light goes green, I zoom down the roads, going around in circles.

My heartbeat speeds up as I quickly pull into the parking lot of Elora Falls High School. We may have graduated two months ago but we still want to use it to our advantage. Curious opportunity lingers within those walls still and I'd be a fool not to even acknowledge it. Speaking of my best friends, there they wait at the front doors, lounging on the brick wall that spells out the school name, large grins on their faces.

"Fuck yeah," I mutter to myself after squealing the tires when rushing into a spot. The car jerks forward as I come to a sudden stop.

I barely shift the Impala's gear into park before I hurry out of the seat, running to greet the people that matter most to me.

3. Who's Missing?

"Nope. This is all wrong. I can't see you if you come out that way. Alright, Crista, can you move it around a bit more to the left?" Irritation coats my throat as I grumble out the words.

We've been at this all morning. Setting up scenes for our upcoming fiction film is such a chore. Nothing is fitting right.

Maybe it's all the leftover props from this year that aren't working together.

Hell, I should be glad the theater department is even allowing us to be in here. The new seniors were taken on a team bonding trip to Alaska so they let us use whatever while they're gone. It's a pretty sweet deal, but boy did I bite off more than I could chew.

Crista shrugs her shoulder and does as I ask. She carefully rotates the cardboard willow tree exactly the way I envisioned. It makes more sense to have the pretty side facing the camera or what's the point of even having these props?

"Where do you want this?" Thomas continues to hold onto a glorious fake green fern.

Oh, I forgot he's standing there.

I shake my head roughly. "Yeah, sorry. Could you put it next to the fireplace? It should go there nicely."

He nods in answer and casually waltzes over with a small smirk. At first, I have no idea why he looks like that until I follow his line of sight. I roll my eyes after realizing he's staring hard at Crista's ass as she bends over to adjust a few fake plants around the tree.

"Unbelievable," I mutter while taking a few steps back to collapse in my makeshift director's chair.

The uneven wooden legs squeak under my weight and the black fabric with my name painted on it in white almost tears as I lean back. I release a shuttering breath once I know the chair won't completely fall apart with me still sitting in it. Dad had saved enough money a while ago that I was able to get some stuff to make the chair. It's not much. But it makes me feel like a real director. I am a *real* director.

After a while, the scene starts to pull together. A clear picture of a homey cottage set in the rural swamps of Louisiana is coming along perfectly. This movie will be epic. It's going to have the right amount of homemade and heart all because of the main character, the hero who dreams of being a Broadway actress who accidentally saves her love interest from a fire-breathing werewolf. Well, at least that's what I'm imagining.

Crista doesn't think it's real enough for the audience.

It's a good thing she is just the writer and not the director. I get the final say, and I say the werewolf is the best part of the movie. Werewolves are awesome.

The doors of the auditorium are thrown open, banging against the walls that are covered in a dark blue velvet material to help the stage lights shine bright.

The noise shocks me into a much straighter position. I shoot angry eyes at whoever it could be that decides to interrupt this precious planning time.

However, my pissed-off expression vanishes at the sight of Bucky strutting down the middle of an aisle lined with dark wood that separates the red audience seats.

A flustered heat rushes to my neck and face. I clear my throat when he gets close enough for us to lock eyes. God, I love his rich brown-green eyes. They shine so wonderfully underneath his harsh lighting that pales me ten times over.

"Hey, man. Where ya been?" Thomas sits on the edge of the stage. A small sweat has broken across his forehead, threatening to slip down the sides of his face. His black hair is plastered to him like a second skin.

Bucky doesn't hesitate to clasp hands with Thomas. They partake in a weird dude handshake that makes me and Crista cringe. Why are guys so odd?

Though my discomfort doesn't stick around to linger when

I notice the bead of salty sweat trailing down the thick artery in Bucky's neck covered by his soft skin.

I wipe my mouth to get rid of any potential drool when Bucky turns his wicked grin towards me. My heart skips a beat. I'm such a sucker, aren't I?

"What's got you all excited?" I'm so thankful that my voice does not falter as I get out of my chair.

Bucky rolls his shoulders. I watch the muscles in his back shift with the movement. They seem too large and luscious underneath his gray shirt.

"And where are the waters that Charlie sent you to go get us?" Crista pushes up the sleeves of her pale pink sweater.

I give her a glare. She ignores me with ease. Typical behavior for her.

"I overheard the radio in Ms. Rudy's class. I guess she turned it on to pass the time while cleaning out her classroom. But it was the local news station blabbing about some missing kid, Peter Williams." Bucky explains as if this is the best news to hit Elora Falls.

Hmm. Peter Williams? Where have I heard that name before?

"The kid who ran the Celebration Club? Nah, he's too good to run away." It's Thomas who jogs my memory.

Vividly, I remember Peter hosting practically every school event. No matter the occasion he managed to convince the school to throw some sort of party. That sweet kid even brought cupcakes for every student's birthday.

It's a wonder how his parents didn't go broke with him funding all of this. Hmm, this news seems a little made-up to me.

"I've had several classes with him. I don't think he ran away

31

either." Crista joins Thomas on the stage edge. Her brows are set in a suddenly furious furrow.

I watch him take her hand and give her knee a comforting squeeze. She welcomes his touch by placing her hand on his tall shoulder. They always seem to be touching each other.

Bucky shakes his head. "No, they aren't talking about him running away. I mean c'mon, we all know him. He would have at least left some sort of note. I think something happened to him."

I inhale deeply and peer around the empty theater. All the spotlights are hitting the center stage, aimed right at the various large props that fit best with the swamp-themed backdrop made from canvas.

"Okay, then what happened to Peter?" Crista presses the unspoken question.

I twirl around with a thought in my mind that has been brewing within me since last night at the movies. My mind is doing its best to come up with explanations that are so far from right.

Carefully, I peel off my raincoat and drape it over the back of my chair. A slight chill races over my exposed arms. I ignore the goosebumps that flourish over my skin.

"You've got your thinking frown. What is it?" Bucky instantly moves to my side, but he fails to comfort me like Thomas always seems to do for Crista.

I don't mind. Him just leaning down to whisper in my ear when no one looks is enough. His very breath hitting my flushed neck does many things to my chest.

I peer at him, feeling a curious glint clatter across my eyes.

"Amy Driscal was sick last night and now suddenly Mr. Perfect... Peter Willams is missing. What if they're connected?"

I cross my arms and tilt my head to ignore Bucky's intense stare.

The three of them groan in unison. Whatever serious tension filled the theater is now all gone thanks to my apparent idiotic thinking. Jeez, I was just trying to make sense of these new situations.

"Yep, let's get back to making this movie." Thomas surprisingly sings when hopping back onto his feet.

Crista follows him with a shake of her head.

Bucky, well, he sighs heavily before roughly patting me on the back. I jerk forward from the force. He leaves my side to help Thomas shuffle a too-heavy pale wood prop dining table before the fireplace. I would have found it overly simple if it weren't for the suspicion that floods my veins.

I take a seat again, my hands finding the script of the movie that isn't complete. Crista still wants to make a few tweaks to it before we can find someone to take the lead. If we wrote it differently, Bucky would have been the star. Perhaps making him the hero's love interest might be a bit much.

It doesn't matter. It's a risk I'm willing to take to destroy my sanity. Anything to make a true name for our film production.

As I continue watching Shocker Pictures set up the scene so I can make sure it will pan out right I can't help but wonder about a few things. Maybe I'm reading too much into this.

Peter was dating this one chick. Her name might have been Candy Perkins. But, he dumped her two weeks before graduation so he could focus on his college fund instead of her strange addiction to sniffing sour candy. She was a weird one and I'm glad she skipped town. I can only hope she made it to a rehabilitation facility for it.

So it doesn't make sense that he just left. It's not Peter. I never truly had many genuine conversations with the kid but from what I saw he was a model citizen. He set an example for lower classmen too. I might be losing my mind prematurely but I smell something strange.

And then there is Amy. I've never seen someone so sick before. There is just too much to try and find the truth about.

A loud thud causes me to unwillingly escape my head. My heart stops beating abruptly.

I see Thomas leaning over the chair he accidentally dropped. His face brought into a panicky sneer. "Sorry."

All of us laugh, quickly forgetting the strangeness that's suddenly brewing in our little town.

Crista shakes her head and places the fake dog next to the table. I almost forgot the hero is supposed to have a dog. Which reminds me of something important. Why can't I ever remember this?

I need to get dog food on the way home for Copper! I really don't want to hear Dad bitch about the bowl being empty again. That's the only reason I even get an allowance.

4. Jake vs Charlie

P ulling into the small parking lot of the Blockbuster is already an absolute thrill. It's a feeling that never lets me down. Not ever. But going inside with my rowdy gang to peer at all the movies and video games is an even more euphoric experience.

Almost like we were born to take over this store. I wouldn't be surprised if that were the case.

There are so many choices to choose from and not enough hours in the night to watch them all. That might be the only flaw this place and we have that we share.

With the film camera clutched in my hands I bend down to closely study the movie titles. Many of them spark interest in me but I'm looking for only one in particular.

I'm not sure where Crista and Thomas went. He most likely has dragged her over to the action movie section. I'm surprised she hasn't complained about looking at it yet. She doesn't enjoy watching fancy explosions with the badass characters walking away from them. I believe it to be the best part about those types of films.

It really sets the stage for true heroism.

After pillaging through the VHS tapes and lucking out on finding anything interesting I stand back up. My breath stalls in my throat when someone's arm gently brushes up against me.

I twist around so fast with my jaw dropped, ready to spill out all kinds of bullshit about creepy men putting their hands where they aren't wanted.

But after catching the most gorgeous smirk from Bucky all my anger just seeps out of me. Damn, he soaks everything I have up like a sponge.

A generous flush travels up my neck, heating my face. I hate when he does that. I get all flustered and he thinks it's so fucking hilarious. Does he know why I act like that when he does stupid shit? I'll bet he has no idea. Well, good for him. He doesn't need to know I feel anything for him.

I rather he be oblivious to my accidental longing stares and lip-biting every time his shirt rises when he stretches in the passenger seat of my car.

I roll my eyes as his subtle laughter drifts away from me. He's heading over to Crista and Thomas, leaving me alone in the horror section of the store. Good. Just the way I like it.

No one in Shocker Pictures enjoys horror like I do. It's my escape and my greatest weapon. I love to be scared. Knowing that none of it is real just gets my heart pumping so fast that sometimes I wonder why I don't pass out.

"Hey, kids! The store closes in ten. Be at the register in five." Chuck calls from the counter. His shrill voice is an odd comfort.

With a shrug of my shoulders, I pick out the first *A Nightmare On Elm Street* again for a fifth time. It's really a habit now to grab it along with the real choice to watch.

On the last Friday of the month, Shocker Pictures has a sleepover at Crista's place. Her mom is always too happy to host such an event. It gives us proper time to watch and enjoy a film without all the fuss at the theater. And tonight will be another hang-out filled with her mom's delicious lasagna and lots of popcorn. Hmm, I can already taste it on my tongue.

"We decided on *Spaceballs* this time!" Thomas shouts from across the store. He must think I'm deaf. What an idiot.

I meet his gaze easily on the count of him being taller than all of us. He just towers over everyone. His eyes glint with mischief. I doubt he will ever mature like a real adult. Maybe that's what I secretly hope for myself. To grow out of this. However, I know that won't ever happen. I'm not going to complain.

I nod my head in answer. It's never a big deal to me about what movie we watch. I want them to choose. They are my friends as well as my crew. Their opinion matters most to me.

Now, I will be the one to pick out the candy. There won't be any argument about that.

"Alright, Chuck. Ring us up and we'll be out of your hair." Bucky leans against the counter. His letterman jacket sleeves glint in the uncomfortable yellow lights that don't do this store justice.

I advert my gaze when he looks at me. There's that damn blush again. Fuck my life.

Crista comes up to my side with a few bags of candy in her hands. I move around to get a better look at her selection. Once I spot Big League Chew I know we're in for a good night. She always knows what to pick out as if I don't ask before we even walk inside the store.

Now that is true friendship.

Thomas starts to chat with Chuck after I place down the movie I was carefully holding onto when the bell above the front door chimes.

All of us turn to look who decides to walk in at the very last minute. How original. As if that has never happened before in cinematic history.

But then my once gleeful mood quickly disappears once I see that it's Jake and his gang that steadily get closer. Oh, great. There goes the neighborhood.

"Shit," Crista mutters. She moves over to where her boyfriend is standing. He instantly wraps his leather-clad arm around her shoulders that's covered in a rather fuzzy floral patterned sweater vest. At least it's not long-sleeved. It's been a very hot day and I would have gotten so pissed if she fainted during rehearsals.

I watch as Bucky tucks a bleached coil behind his ear. A strange glint catches my attention. Are those rings on his fingers? When did he start wearing silver?

"Well, looks like we ran into Shocker Pictures and their new member." Jake grins. His chubby nose wrinkles as he shows off his gold tooth. As if he's intimidating.

His goons snicker around him as their eyes latch on Bucky.

My brows furrow in confusion. But as quickly as that expression comes it vanishes once I cross my arms. My red coat rubs over my skin with the movements.

Jake's muddy brown eyes meet mine. They're dull and void of any joy. What a punk.

"What do you want?" My voice carries through the empty store with strict confidence.

The newest arrivals frown at me with harsh distaste. Good because I don't like them either. And Jake should know that already.

Jake shrugs. His glare rolls around the store and finally lands back on Bucky. Without much thought put into it, I step forward, stopping in front of him. I know where this conversation is going to go before Jake even opens his mouth. He's not all big and bad like he thinks he is.

His eyes crinkle with that cringe-worthy smile of his.

"Just didn't think the queer football star of Elora Falls would ever be caught hanging out with you fuckers." And just like that, all my rage from earlier rushes back into my chest. It feels like I have heartburn now.

I sense Bucky shift awkwardly behind me. Yeah, the mood is ruined.

Okay, yes. There have been rumors that Bucky hooked up with Jeremy Logs in the boys' locker room before the final game. And? Me and my friends have always known this about Bucky since he first joined the Shocker Pictures. It doesn't make a shit to me. It has nothing to do with his outstanding skills on the field.

From what Bucky has told me, his father could care less about his sexuality as long as it doesn't interfere with his sports. So far, he's gotten eight scholarship offers from schools across the country. Now that is top dog shit!

Jake's irritating snort fills my ears. "Yeah, coach caught them locking lips in the shower. And you'd think the best player on the team was into pussy like the rest of them. I'm surprised they didn't get so far as to tickle each other's cocks."

They all begin to laugh like it's the funniest speech they've ever heard.

He has done stupid shit like this since we got to high school. He and his gang like to pick on the weak and torment the popular. No one truly won while in his presence.

I've had enough of him and his patchy red beard. Fuck this freak.

"Alright, that's it!" My vision is clouded by a red haze in a matter of moments.

With one large step forward, I'm swinging my tight fist into his nose. A crack fills the air. Then everyone breaks out into a brawl.

"Fuck yeah!" Thomas shouts and strikes the nearest man of Jake's buddies.

I can hear Crista sigh heavily before kicking someone in the knee.

Jake manages to swipe me across the jaw. I jerk to the side with blood filling my mouth. He doesn't get a chance to smirk when I hawk a spit full of my fresh blood. It lands in his gaping mouth and all over his face. Nice.

"Fuck!" He screeches before grabbing a chunk of my hair. It might have been a good idea to braid it back before walking into the Blockbuster tonight.

"Damnit." Bucky seethes as I get punched in the gut.

He knows not to get involved like the rest of us. I won't let him lose his scholarships over some petty fighting. It's my pleasure to beat this prick's ass anyway.

"Just called the cops, idiots." Chuck tries to raise his voice but I barely hear him over the ringing in my ears.

Jake takes me by the throat. I claw at his hands. Seeing Crista out of the corner of my eyes currently biting someone's arm only fuels my fight. And then there's Thomas who tosses another guy into the nearest case filled with movie taps. It crashes around us. The tapes land in multiple thuds, bouncing roughly off the tiled floor.

If we aren't banned by the end of this then I'll lick my foot for the hell of it. And if I'm banned then Jake will really be dead by the end of the month.

Bucky leans against the counter still with his arms crossed and a scowl set on his face. By the way his sweet eyes narrow at me, I can tell he wants to throw a punch or two. Well, he shouldn't worry because I will always have his back. No matter who the fuck's nose I have to break.

In a matter of seconds, police sirens trail down the street.

"Shit." Jake curses before shoving me harshly into the floor, making the back of my head collide with the solid floor.

I groan before leaning over on my side to see him and his gang rush out of the front door, the bell singing loudly as they do.

Crista comes over with watery eyes. The skin of her left cheek had been split. Blood trails down her face. Damn, she got hit pretty good too. But she knows it was worth it. We all protect each other from anything. She helps me sit up.

41

Thomas limps to her side and reaches down to yank me up on my feet.

"Now that was awesome. Where did you learn to punch like that?" Thomas asks as if he doesn't already know the answer to it. It's not my first fight with Jake and I don't think it will be my last either. I have a habit of throwing the first punch. I like the adrenaline rush it gives me.

"Ah, you know, I like a bit of trouble." I indulge him anyway, simultaneously locking my gaze with Bucky's.

With a shrug of my shoulders, I feel brand new. I peer around my friends to look at Chuck and give him my best smile.

"Don't worry. You're safe now." The joke continues to encourage our laughter as we hurry out of the door with the movies and snacks, leaving poor Chuck with a ruined store.

I'll come back tomorrow to help him clean up the mess. It's the least I could do since I started the fight. But damn did that feel so good.

Hoots and hollers full of pride engulf the inside of the car. The shout of the engine only causes my friends to burst into song. They belt out lyrics for "Don't Stop Believing" by Journey. It's a funny coincidence that it so happens to be playing on the radio as I twist the nob on.

I back out in a flash once the blue and red lights of the cop cars get too close for comfort. I can't have Sheriff Osburn ratting me out to my dad. I don't think I could handle his rare disappointment.

A bright smile tugs on my lips, but I hold back as my hand bumps into Bucky's as he adjusts the air vent.

My breath hitches as he gives me a fierce wink. It doesn't take long for that smile to break through and my foot to hit the gas peddle.

We speed down the street with the cops arriving at the Blockbuster. Once we arrive at Crista's place we'll be able to smother ourselves with these spoils of war... Well, the movies and candy.

5. R.I.P Peter

Our victory doesn't last very long when we walk through the front door. Crista's mom scolds us so badly that I think Thomas is going to puke from nerves. She makes sure he gets the extra attention like that. She keeps him on his toes.

However, her dad steps in and shooes us away. I'm grateful for their strange marriage dynamic. It's like good cop and bad cop in detective movies. It works well for them.

As soon as our feet step foot on Crista's pale blue carpet we all heave a sigh of relief. I flop onto her bed which was neatly made up with a soft pink comforter. Thomas moves over to the large TV that sits in the middle of the back wall and fixes up the movie. Bucky does what he normally does when we come over. That is him laying out the candy in a large bowl, mixing the sugary snacks, and discarding the plastic bags into the trash bin.

I might study him do this a little too closely.

I sit on the bed and watch him do this while Crista gathers the blankets from the nearby basket. It's a lovely sight to see his muscles flex when he rips the bags open. Sometimes he has to use his perfect teeth. I rather like it when he almost growls in frustration when they sometimes don't open in a clean motion.

Damn, I'm the freak of this odd group.

"Miss Director, I believe we have a new movie to investigate." Bucky finishes up and takes a seat beside me.

"I think I have to agree." I gently smirk before grabbing the TV remote.

Thomas strips off his jacket and jumps onto the bed, instantly wrapping his arms around Crista. Her giggles warm my heart as I click play.

It's Fridays like these that make me want to shout from the rooftops that I have the best of friends in the entire world. We all fit together. I never want this little tradition of ours to end.

And yet despite my wish, I know it will.

As all four of us lean back on the tall brown headboard of the bed and snuggle into the blankets I can't help but feel worried.

Sure, I shouldn't with the hilarious parody of *Star Wars*

playing on the wide screen.

Ever since going to the movies I've had this strange feeling. Of course, it goes away each time I'm with my friends as we prep for our film. That leaves no room in my mind to think of other things. But when I get home and sit alone in my room I come up with all these crazy ideas about why my entire being feels so off.

This is one of those times I'm afraid. I can feel my mind begging me to come up with crazy conclusions to my self-made theories. They never do any good. So why do I expect them to now?

I must be furrowing my brows hard enough to catch Bucky's attention because his calloused yet gentle pointer finger carefully rubs the crease between them, smoothing my skin.

A careful smile spreads across my face as I peer at him. There is a slight sparkle in his eyes that I want to try my fucking best to ignite into dazzling flames. Is that so wrong?

"If you keep thinking like that, then your head will explode." He leans close enough to whisper.

Despite my sudden flush, I roll my eyes. "You have no idea."

Bucky chuckles softly. I don't even notice his arm wrap around me until his hand gives my shoulder a firm squeeze. How did I not feel him?

Crista and Thomas are engaged in their own conversation about the quirky dialogue of the movie. Their small arguing is enough to keep them distracted from us. Good. I like it when it's just me and him.

"I would if you finally decide to spill all your dark deadly secrets." The corners of his thick lips inch higher and higher with each word.

My heart ticks a messy rhythm. Somehow my fingers lace

with his on my shoulder. His grip on me tightens along with my chest.

I open my mouth to most likely utter nonsense when a loud knock on the door breaks up this brewing tension between us. Damn.

In an instant, I'm ripping away from him and jumping off the bed to open the door with a slight frown on my face.

The irritated expression hurries to simmer into one of surprise. "Hey, Mr. Fisher."

"Dad?" Crista jerks to stand off the bed. Her face is fully flushed. I bet they've been making out for a few minutes while me and Bucky were conversing. Bastards. I'm so glad I was not watching that happen. I would have barfed up all the candy I ate a while ago.

"Hi, kids. Uh, we want you guys to come downstairs. There is something you might wanna hear." His furious red brows raise towards his patchy hairline.

I just kind of stand there as he slowly walks away, sticking his trembling hands into the pockets of his brown slacks.

The feeling comes rushing back into my body. Nerves trail down my spine. I bite the inside of my lip to keep my grim frown at bay.

Instead of showing any ounce of the fear that swells within me, I twist around to face them.

Bucky comes to my side, his gaze seeped in worry. I force myself not to acknowledge the way he looks at me. I know it's not more than a friendly amount of concern. I can handle him not loving me like I love him.

Thomas takes Crista's hands gently.

With me leading them, we gradually descend the stairs. The hallway lights have been dimmed. I'm not sure why this freaky ambiance is necessary. It only makes me more suspicious of what they want to tell us. It sure as hell can't be anything good.

My feet covered in cozy black socks meet the hardwood floor of the kitchen. There sits Crista's parents at the kitchen table. Their faces show many emotions that can't quite fuse properly. Like one is fighting the other for dominance.

I cross my arms as Mrs. Fisher takes a stand, pulling the dark green cardigan closer around herself. Her pale strawberry hair has been braided over her shoulder. Her pale skin only causes her bright blue eyes to shimmer in a brutal way.

We aren't going to like this one bit.

The older woman clears her throat. The action causes my heart to skip a beat. I allow my lips to curl into a grimace from the disturbing noise.

"The police have been calling the homes of students who might have been close to Peter Williams during school."

Shit. Shit!

My breaths come and go a little quicker. I see Crista out of the corner of my eye shift uncomfortably into Thomas's chest. She had the most classes with Peter. They collaborated on the morning announcements more than once as well. Crista likes to do all sorts of creative writing as strong practice for our movie scripts.

"So, what's up?" Thomas shrugs his shoulder. A thing he does when he gets nervous. It happened every time he was called on the intercom to visit the principal's office.

I gulp after Bucky takes hold of the back of my shirt. Now that is new on his part. He isn't the obvious touchy type which is such a bummer because I've dreamed of licking his juicy abs. Wait, no. I can think about that wicked fever dream later.

I force the vivid image out of my head when tears slip down

Mrs. Fisher's face.

"Well, they found his body out near the border of town. His family wanted his friends to know that the funeral will be sometime next week." Mr. Fisher steps up to take his wife's hands.

This is a small town. People talk and spread gossip. But every death, every heartache, affects us all. It's not surprising that Crista's parents are emotional over this. I can hear her gently cry into Thomas's shoulder. I watch him weave his fingers through her thick red hair to soothe her growing sobs.

I roll my shoulder to try and shake that feeling away, but it only gains strength with my fight. If any one of us has to be the token strong one it should be me. It has to.

Bucky moves around to stand beside me. Our hands graze each other's. No matter how much I want to take that hand of his that easily can toss a football, I can't. It's not the time.

Mr. Fisher urges us to return to our movie and just settle ourselves. Reluctantly, I tread up the stairs behind them. My feet get heavier with each step I take. It's never a good feeling when your shoulders hunch from all the annoying sorrow and many daunting questions you have just begging to be answered.

Getting back to the room is just bonkers. None of this is rad at all.

Thomas gives Crista a fierce kiss before grabbing a spare blanket and pillow off the floor. He walks out the door and past with me sporting a sad smile. This guy is not one to show too much emotion unless it comes to my best friend. She is the most likely to break under pressure. But her writing is the best of the best and I think all of us want to see her smile. She is the sunshine that dwells in Shocker Pictures. Her bright energy will prove useful in the future of this company.

Her harsh sniff encourages me to go to her. It's an instinct only the closest of friends can have for each other. I haven't seen a lot of it during our time in school. Most of the popular dicks ratted each other every chance they got. I've witnessed a few ugly fights and I've joined in a lot too.

Bucky lingers beside me. He visibly hesitates to take a step forward. Once I give him a slight smile it's enough for him to follow after Thomas with a pillow and blanket of his own.

When their hefty footsteps start down the stairs I finally exhale, forcing all the building tension in my slightly hunched shoulders out into the open where it can no longer hurt me.

My heart splinters as Crista's quiet cries flutter around the room. With a heavy sigh, I close the bedroom door and join her on the bed.

Her trembling form melts against me, letting me wrap her in my arms like a stuffed bear.

"W-What's happening h-here?" Her small hiccups brought on by her soft sobs pinch the insides of my ears.

My mouth opens but words fail to come out. What do I tell her? I have no clue what's going on in this town. I'm used to it being full of quirky people who sometimes can't stay out of others' business.

My eyes roll with sudden irritation. I have to tell her something or else her tears will only pour harder. I love her to death but damn can this chick can cry like a newborn baby fresh out of the womb.

I gently rub her arm in a soothing motion, doing everything to will her into a much-needed sleep. "I don't have the answer to that, Cris."

And I hate that more than anything.

I didn't stay asleep for very long.

After getting Crista to shut her eyes finally, I guess I did too. But then a nightmare gave me a startling fright, causing me to jolt awake with my arms wrapped around her. My grip on her was so tight that her breathes were slightly strangled. I quickly release her.

Sweat drips down my forehead as I recall the bad dream. All I can grasp onto before it fades away completely is Peter with green snot dripping down his nose just like Amy at the theater.

That is very odd. I can't explain why my mind would even conjure up something like that. It could be the voice in my head trying to convince me that there is something going on in this town. I have a pretty damn good feeling that things are going to get worse. But I doubt the two incidents are connected in that specific way. I'm not that delusional.

It isn't easy to keep secrets in this place. Eventually, everyone will know your darkest things.

With a curt jerk of my head, I gently crawl off the bed. My feet still hidden underneath fuzzy socks glide across her fluffy carpet. It takes me a few moments to gather my bearings. My head swarms with an upcoming headache. I stifle a groan as I make my way to the guest bathroom in the hallway. I could use the one connected to her room but I don't want the light to wake her. Though, I'm more than sure it won't since the blinking TV is still on blaring bright ass end-movie credits across the room.

There is a throbbing ache in my lip. I won't be surprised if I see it swollen and purple in the mirror. I think my nose is broken too.

I'm halfway down the hall when I spot Bucky sleeping at the top of the stairs. His head leans against the wall and his shoulders are covered in a pale green blanket with white airplanes dotting over it.

He looks so peaceful. That little crease on his forehead is gone along with his usual noble guy act. I'm tempted to put the loose curl over his eyes behind his ear.

My lips beg to lift into a smile. I feel new blood leaking down my chin.

Once I rush to the bathroom I close the door quietly behind me and flick the light switch.

Ugly yellow lights on top of the mirror temporarily blind me. Once my tired eyes adjust I get a clear image of my horrid face.

My stomach grumbles uncomfortably due to the person staring back at me. My hair is dull and too yellow, having lost most of its natural volume and little remains of the hairspray I used earlier today.

Dark purple bags kiss the angry skin under my reddish eyes. My bottom lip is split deeper than I thought. I take a shaky finger, lean forward, and too suddenly peel the flesh apart.

A hiss seeps out of me as I get a gruesome view of the pink tissue of the lip. It barely glistens due to being held apart the whole night. If I don't find some way to pinch it together then it will be like this permanently. I can't have that. What happens if I get famous and have to walk the red carpet for directing a killer movie?

Yeah, no thanks.

I rummage through the medicine cabinet kept behind the mirror. A few bandages are scattered on the bottom shelf. After ripping them open I join the torn pieces together and basically tape them.

Once I'm satisfied with my strange medical work I take a wash rag off the top to the toilet, damping it to wipe my face clean of all the crusty blood.

By the time I finish, I'm totally exhausted. With a deep sigh, I exit the bathroom, only to give a startled gasp at the sight of Bucky leaning against the stair railing, his hazel eyes pinned on me.

I cross my arms while getting myself together, forcing my fear deeper into my belly.

"Shouldn't you be sleeping down on the couch with Thomas?" I keep my voice low.

He gives a lousy shrug.

I roll my eyes and begin to walk away. He moves in a blur to grasp my elbow. His touch on me causes my heart to stutter. It's too late in the night for my feelings to squirm.

"You good?" His words do something to me and encourage me to give him a look. Too bad I can't smirk at him with the four bandaids I have on my mouth.

My silence urges him to speak again. "Charlie, are you okay?"

I peer up at him, trying my best to be unbothered. I want to walk away with my signature smirk and act like everything in the world is fine. But am I actually fine? I'm not. He doesn't

53

THE MUSH

need to know that.

"Jake and his buddies are fucktards. He had it coming. It's not the first time he and I got into it. I'm alright." My attitude doesn't really match my feelings. It's the best I can do.

I don't wait for him to scold me. He always makes sure I know that my occasional bad behavior will get me nowhere in life. I think he just wishes he has the balls to do shit. That's okay because I love him too much to let him get his hands dirty. Maybe one day he will see me and love me back. Until then, me and my busted lip will be quiet.

I tear away from him and head back to the room. Despite my heart wanting, begging me to, I don't turn back to see the sad expression I know he has on his wonderful face.

He doesn't need me to hold him back from greatness.

6. That Green Goop Again

Dressing in black never was and never will be my thing.

The color is a sign of heartbreak and darkness. Whoever decided it's required to be worn during funerals should have been castrated. Because seeing waves of grim faces shrouded in icky sadness certainly does prove to be depressing. I only feel irritated that I couldn't be the one to grasp the fucker's balls and twist them off myself.

All these gloomy frowns remind me of the last funeral I attended. My mother's.

Watching the closest friends of Peter Williams carry his light brown wooden casket to the hole in the ground brings back a memory I wish I could destroy.

The tears streaming down their faces are shiny due to the late afternoon sunlight that cascades over them. Carefully, they lower Peter's slowly deteriorating corpse into the moist ground. His mother and father's loud sobs fill the silence that does its best to consume everything.

They're sitting in the front row in distinct white lawn chairs so people can pick them out of the crowd. A way to lure the attention whores who must put their two senses in about all of this. I don't understand why they have to be so assertive in events that have nothing to do with them.

And yet they are never too far away. The human vultures linger close, waiting for their chance to give condolences and such. It's pathetic really.

Not many people showed up other than these odd folks to my surprise. Shocker Pictures along with Peter's buddies had been the only ones to get an invite. Others have simply stumbled their way into the service. I'm still not sure why us, why me.

The funeral officiant limps to the small podium near the hole in the ground. From the looks of it, it's Mr. Jack who runs the only church in town. The poor old fart never goes outside unless it's for events like this. His trembling wrinkled hands grip the edges of the stand. He clears his throat to grab our attention.

Crista squeezes my knee in response.

It takes everything in me not to flinch at her sudden touch.

I've been sitting between her and Bucky for the last two hours. Having to endure many family speeches that brought me to tears with him so close to me has been extremely aggravating. His hand brushes against my thigh more times than usual. My skin itches for him to find a way to touch me under the long black velvet skirt that rests just above my ankles.

God, he shouldn't look so mouth-watering in his all-black suit with his wild curls pulled back in a loose bun at the base of his wonderful head.

Thomas felt that his leather jacket was enough black. However, the bright red shirt underneath it really deters the aesthetic.

Though I can see he wears a particular shade of red to match Crista's lipstick. She wears that specific red whenever she wants to make a statement. I'm just not sure what that is just yet. At least it goes wonderful with her billowing black dress with puffy long lace sleeves. She's a true vision and puts my plain dark grey t-shirt to shame.

This was all I had to wear to this thing. I do my best to avoid colors that make me want to sit in a dark room and cry like a fucking baby.

The elderly man delivers the tragic eulogy and lets the guy in the back know to play Peter's favorite song.

My chest aches when 'Another One Bites the Dust' by Queen starts to play on the boombox. I hate the irony of that.

I didn't know goody-two-shoes Peter was into such music. I always figured he preferred jazz. He sure did have the perfect curly blonde hair that hinted towards it. Sometimes I thought he walked straight out of the twenties when he dressed in

57

those brown slacks and adorable sweater vests. Damn, I never thought I'd lose a fellow classmate so early in life. It doesn't seem real.

The song is over too quickly. People stand and crowd the parents like greedy hyenas. No matter how close all these people are they still prove to be fucking leaches.

We get on our feet as well. However, none of us make a move to give our condolences. We don't possess the right to do so.

Bucky rolls his shoulders back. The blonde highlights in his hair shine with the dying light. I do everything it takes not to groan in satisfaction at the sight. This isn't the time or place to admire this man.

Crista takes mine and Thomas's hand, her fingers lacing with ours.

"What are we supposed to do now?" Her voice trembles. She's been a crying mess all morning that you'd think she was the one to lose a family member and not Peter's parents losing a child.

My eyes roll with ease. "Go home and forget this ever happened."

Not the best thing to do after our friend was buried.

"C'mon, let's get some pizza and Coke." Bucky's suggestion has my stomach gurgling.

I toss my thick braid over my shoulder as we file out of the row.

Before we even start heading towards the cemetery parking lot a sharp shout rings out into the air.

Due to my stalling heart, I stumble into the back of Bucky. Crista follows suit and crashes into me. We're like playing dominos on family game nights. I think Thomas actually collapses into the nearest chair.

His surprised huff is quite funny. I'd laugh if it wasn't for this odd flush of silence that tries its best to coat the sadness of this day.

"Sorry," I mutter to Bucky before stepping on the tips of my toes to figure out where the scream originated from. I use his shoulders to give myself a little more height. I may also be digging my fingers into the fabric of his jacket on purpose just to feel him close.

Everyone remains as they wonder what's happening. Their clueless eyes and gaping mouths all seem to point to the small group that hovers around the cemetery sidewalk. Huh?

To get a better look I push around my friends. No one stops me as I peer at the older woman who tries to calm down a young guy who is drenched in sweat. I don't recognize him. He must be a cousin of Peter from out of town.

His pale skin is rapidly shifting to a nasty shade of green. Small open wounds are covering his neck and exposed arms. I swear they're leaking a gross green slime. I've seen this before!

How could I have not noticed him earlier?

How did he get so sick in such a short time? He couldn't have been here longer than a week. There is definitely something wrong here.

My eyes widen as he collapses to his shaky knees. His hoarse cough morphs into gurgles. Thick green puke shoots out of his mouth and red irritated nostrils. I gulp down my own bile that attempts to escape me. This shit is disgusting.

"No, you don't!" Crista grabs me by my shirt and jerks me back into her chest.

I fail at shrugging her arms off of me as she wraps them around my thin waist.

"Good call, Love Bug." Thomas pats her on the shoulder.

The action almost makes me swoon for them, but the evolving scene before me continues to possess my full undivided attention.

Sirens from cops and an ambulance interrupt my crazy thoughts.

The crowd around the guy grows before people push everyone else back to the parking lot. Sheriff Osburn directs Peter's parents away from the scene. His deputy sports a sweaty forehead as he ushers the medical team to the suffering boy.

Bucky steps in to intertwine his fingers with mine, forcing me to walk away from this madness that I desperately want to explore.

I'm surprised that drool isn't leaking down my chin when the guy shouts in agony. I just want to see what's happening. Maybe that's what makes me a sicko. I don't care.

I now regret allowing Thomas to leave the video camera in the car. This would have been such a fantastic shot.

A shocking idea forms in my mind by the time we reach my Impala.

Once ripping away from the boy I love too deeply I skip ahead and block their path, leaving the rest of the funeral service behind us.

Crista crosses her arms with an irritated sigh. Her boyfriend shoves his hands into his pant pockets, his thick brows raised in suspicion. And then there is Bucky leaning against the driver's side door with a disappointed look on his beautiful face. I know that expression more than I'd like to.

"What?" I ask in a too-highly-pitched tone.

Even I can hear my sudden unnecessary excitement.

Crista scoffs. "We know that look. Hell, you invented the look of a Bad Idea, Char."

I roll my eyes sharply. A grin of disbelief crawls on my lips.

"Just say what you're thinking so we can get this over with." Thomas really should keep his big mouth shut.

I draw in a deep breath and make sure to lock eyes with each of them.

"I know you saw that guy back there. He looks just like Amy did in the theater. This can't be a coincidence. God, I think that's what happened to Peter. It makes sense." My smile stretches wide as I explain my thoughts to them.

They stand there, staring at me as if my head was chopped off by a dull butter knife. It might as well have been.

I raise my hands as my questions have suddenly been answered by whoever lingers above us in the clouds. Well, that is a little dramatic.

"All of it's connected. I just can't figure out why or how except for the fact they all have been crazy sick. Something that not even Mr. Freddy could imagine and he is one gross fuck." It's not helping my favor to mention a movie villain now. But anything that will help my growing case I'll take.

Thomas shakes his head, dark hair falling across his forehead in spite of how hard Crista tried caking it back with sticky hair gel that smells like sour green apples.

"Okay, does this mean you're officially going nuts?"

"Oh, shove it, douche!"

Bucky jolts off the side of my car to push me away from Thomas before I can scratch his pretty face. I didn't even realize that I stepped forward with my clenched fist raised ready for the punch. "That's enough."

With a huff, I move away and cross my arms.

I hear my friends sigh. However, I can't determine if their sounds are fueled by disappointment or anger. It doesn't

61

matter in the end.

"I get what you're trying to tell us, really I do. But, Charlie… This is too much. If you even think about going down this road we might not like what you find." Crista always seems to have a level head. Too bad I don't have a single rational bone in my body to agree with her.

Strangely, tears of frustration prick at my eyes. I'm not sure why I so roughly believe in the unordinary and weird. To them, I'm grasping dangerously short straws. But how can they understand if they continue to belittle my theory?

They just need to open their eyes a little wider.

"Fine. I'll drop it. End of discussion." My rare anger gets the best of me.

I give an agitated sniffle before rushing into the car. I wait for the rest to slowly follow in my steps. Then I zoom us out of the parking lot like a bat out of hell. I almost want to smile at the phrase that my dad uses too often. However, I refuse to even blink in a barely relaxed way.

Crista gives my shoulder a firm squeeze before she and Thomas flee the car once I park in her driveway. She notices when I flinch at her touch again. I don't mean to. Knowing her she won't bring it up the next time we see each other. She's caring in that way.

The car is consumed with such thick tension that it can be cut in half with scissors, leaving me and Bucky to wallow in the mess I didn't anticipate creating.

It gets worse when I don't fully pull into his dad's driveway. For some reason, I always get an odd feeling when I'm near Bucky's place. Maybe it's due to his dad's bizarre sports ritual. He never goes without talking about football, basketball, and soccer. No matter when or where he is he just has to tell someone about sports.

And on the rare occasions when I see him he always starts a conversation about fast mail delivery records as a way to connect with me. He's a strange man.

I leave the Impala running. Bucky hesitates to get out of the passenger seat. His eyes are on me, but this time they feel warm. He wants to tell me something.

"Charlie?" His voice is a soft blanket to my heart.

I don't let myself dive into the perfect soul entrapped in his eyes.

"Yes?" My choice shakes.

He inhales deeply, preparing himself to give me a real talking to. I can't say for sure if I'm ready to hear whatever it may be.

"We're just looking out for you. We care so much for you. I care for you. None of us want to see you waste these last few weeks on a disappointing ghost chase. Alright?" No matter how hard I try to be bold and independent, I will forever do what's best for my friends. They come first before everything else.

But what am I supposed to do when they each leave me and this little town? I'm not ready to find out.

No words flutter off my tongue. All I manage to do is nod.

Bucky reluctantly gets out of the car.

I don't linger around to watch him look back at me as the tears from earlier finally drip down my face in slow rivers.

7. I Smell Something Fishy

Who said plotting a movie was hard? Because I find immense joy in putting scenes together like puzzle pieces in the late morning on the back porch. Everything that builds in my mind falls in line with such ease. It's epic magic only I can wield. The script that Crista wrote is absolutely rad. I can't wait to start rehearsing the scenes after we host auditions for the lead.

Not just anyone can be starring in the same movie as Bucky. They need to be perfect.

My dad had built a picnic table with two benches from a kit he bought at Home Depot the last time he had to go out of town for work. Ever since I've spent much of my time outside facing the grueling forest that surrounds Elora Falls.

Being able to see the tall winding cedar trees covered in soft layers of moss influences me to be in a good mood. And of course, the sun catches on the pale red cap mushrooms perfectly, illuminating the pearl-colored spots on their tops. The other various fungi also seem to thrive here as well. The constant rain fuels the moist ground so much that it sours.

The stench of the damp earth wafts into my nostrils on the slightly chilled wind. It may be summer but it's not hot.

I inhale the sharp smell. The sting in my sinuses indicates that this is exactly what I need to unwind.

The dull-pointed pencil in my hands glides off the paper of my rough composition notebook that's covered in graphic stickers. Most are for horror movies and others are for the special fantasy movies that I hold close to my heart.

My loose blonde curls sway in the breeze as I lean closer to my current page. The lines I wrote from the script match with the corresponding scene I sketched out. I'm not much of a drawer so they look quite horrific. It doesn't truly matter as long as my crew gets the picture.

They usually can make out my vision despite all the rugged pen marks.

My certain flow of planning is interrupted by the front door slamming open and crashing against the foyer wall.

I jerk with a start when I peer through the massive wall at the back of the house that is made of large windows and catch

65

sight of my dad hauling brown paper bags inside.

With a wicked eye-roll, I'm up on my feet, my fluffy socks sticking to the wooden wraparound porch floor as I make my way back inside the cool house.

"I could have helped." I give a gentle chuckle when he places them on the kitchen island.

They land on the countertop with a sharp thud.

Dad shakes his head. "Nope. I got it covered."

How typical. He never lets me help despite my occasional begging. That man refuses to rely on others and I understand why more than I'd like.

After placing my hands on my hips and giving him a stern glare he shrugs.

However, my personal glee slips away as I notice the sweat dripping down the side of his face.

"What's wrong?" His forehead is crinkled.

My dad takes a seat on the nearest stool and wipes his face clean with the bottom of his light blue flannel. "There's been talk. I overheard Ms. Noll in the market. She told Mr. Patts about more people showing up at the clinic with bizarre green wounds on them. Others have said the CDC has been called in. I have no idea if those people will be showing up here for a flue. But, who knows what will happen if this thing continues to spread."

I know I heard him right. My brain processes the information and instantly lights up like the Fourth of July for all the wrong reasons.

It takes immense strength to bite back my knowing grin. I knew something fishy was going on! I wonder if people will believe me now.

Instead of gloating over this, I shrug my shoulders, faking

that I have no idea of what he's talking about. If he knew I was already snooping around with these ideas then he'd have my head. I wouldn't be able to watch a movie for a week. He'd literally take every single one of my VHS tapes like he did back when I was in junior high. It had been the most tragic experience. The worst grounding to ever live.

"Do you think it's… I don't know… Food poisoning?" If I get him to elaborate a little more then I can dig deeper with my own investigation that will be placed in full swing sooner rather than later.

This time I will be telling Shocker Pictures and they won't shoot me down again. I'll show them it's all really happening.

His random snort in between his nervous laughter almost makes me want to ask something else that doesn't involve whatever this is. Almost.

He wipes stray tears from his eyes as he says, "From what people are saying, this is some kind of disease. That's why the doc up at the clinic demanded the CDC hurry their asses up here. They should be here by the end of the week if Elora Falls is lucky."

I want to ask what kind of disease they suspect but I get deterred when the home phone on the far side of the kitchen rings.

My dad lifts his head sharply, slowly getting back on his usually aching feet to reach it. His face scrunches as the other person on the other end of the line tells him something.

All I can do is stand there, impatiently tapping my feet on the floor as his expression is consumed with pure worry.

An annoying nagging in my chest does its best to tear my spirit apart. I won't let it drill into the little self-respect I have these days.

As soon as he hangs up the entire house is lit with unease. Anxiously, I rub my elbows. "Who was that?"

"The mayor's assistant. She's been calling the Elora Falls residents who haven't left town yet on their summer vacations. The mayor wants to host a town meeting in April Square to talk about the recent sick cases." He scratches his chin too slowly for my liking.

I make a huff before addressing this.

"Well, since the meetings usually only take place a week before Christmas, this has got to be serious." And like always, Dad doesn't disagree. I detest that too.

The moment all one hundred and thirty-eight of us arrive at the south side of April Square we're separated into five lines, made to stand six feet apart.

Older teens and young adults have been smushed together far away from each other. A lot of the little kids cry silently as they watch their mommies and daddies be kept across from them. Others are complaining about this ridiculous misuse of power from Mayor Sparks.

Sheriff Osburn orders the other officers to make sure no one panics too much and accidentally hurts the nurses. From what I can see Deputy Cain is keeping an eye out for the mayor. Jeez, this is nuts.

They don't enjoy being told to linger in a line while the clinic nurses check people for fevers and skin lesions. What a bunch of losers.

And yet as they voice their rather brutal complaints about the long wait to the front of the line, I wonder how we got to this point.

My mind is infiltrated with little bitty pieces that were and still are collecting in a big ass pile. They're snippets of what happened with poor Amy at the theater and others for Peter and his now newly dead cousin.

I think it's safe to say that the CDC coming here can either go two ways: all of us are so fucking screwed or something is going on that needs to be covered up. From the sounds of it, both options can really end the same way. Disaster.

I've seen a lot of movies in my young life. All ranging from pretty mystical fantasy to wicked horror. They seem to have a few key aspects in common. Discovering and somehow disposing of a villain being the main one.

But that's insane to apply that to this type of situation. Maybe my crew, Shocker Pictures, is right about me thinking too much into this. There can't be any evil plan set up by the bad guy. It's just in the movies. Right? I'm going to let that fishy theory simmer a while longer until true evidence appears before me.

"Open your mouth and lift your tongue for me." Nurse Ally, an older woman with pale blonde hair does her best to smile at me.

69

I hadn't realized I was walking ahead to reach the end of the line. I must have gotten lost in my crazy ideas again.

"Sure." I do what she asks. She places a freshly sanitized thermometer under my tongue. It presses against the back of my jaw. It's an uncomfortable thirty seconds.

My hands tremble at my sides as I quickly glance around the rest of us. The cops have bright yellow hospital masks on their faces and are handing them out to those who have already had their temperatures taken.

"Okay, now can you lift your shirt and move your sleeves? I need to check your skin." She tells me after ripping the medical device out of my mouth a little too harshly.

I rub my tingling jaw and push the sleeves up of my red raincoat. It had lightly sprinkled on us as me and my dad left the house leaving the material slippery.

Her cold fingers gently prod at me. The small lines crease across her forehead as she concentrates on the examination.

I give an irritated huff when she accidentally tickles my sides.

She clears her throat before straightening her scrub top. "Clear!"

Without waiting for her permission, I stalk forward and rip the mask from the cop's hands. I don't know his name. I don't care about it either.

He guides me to the many rows of white lawn chairs that have also been spread out across the square. I'm guessing the mayor bought them all from the supermarket for this.

After taking a closer look at the people already sitting down I spot my friends in various places.

Crista is sitting with her parents more towards the front. From what I can tell, Thomas is with his mom on the far right. And after I step on my tippy toes I find Bucky with his dad at the very back. I hate that we are spread out like this. We are better and stronger when we face things together.

I'm more than sure it's the universe's way of saying 'fuck you' to me.

"Keep moving." The same cop who gave me my mask that feels itchy on my face comes over to usher me forward. How rude.

I curtly roll my eyes. "Got it."

I wait a while near the middle row of chairs for my dad. It takes him a few moments to notice me. Once he does his worried expression shifts into one of relief.

"Let's go sit somewhere, Char." My dad almost wraps his arm around my shoulder. But the cop that obnoxiously clears his throat deters him from doing so.

Right. Whatever this sickness is must be contagious through physical contact.

It doesn't take long for the seats to fill when we take ours right in the center.

A small stage has been set up at the front. Many of the mayor's officials are running around up there with sweaty faces. I don't believe it's from the sickness. They always seem to be stressed when he makes them do things. From what I've seen during my childhood he is damn bossy.

I see him out of the corner of my eyes. His frothy white hair and thick mustache are unforgettable.

His bad knee somehow manages to get him up the stairs in a short time. His assistant holds his signature speech cards. Of course, he has his speech planned. He's too much of a control freak to wing it. During the first semester of school, he likes to host an assembly about safety and good deeds. It's literally the same every time.

71

The dingy wooden podium he approaches creaks when he rests his thick arms on the top. Sweat drips down his face, soaking his medical mask. It's not a great summer here so far.

His hoarse voice on the count of smoking too many cigarettes booms over our heads. "It's times like these that bring the people of Elora Falls together."

I notice my dad fidgeting with his fingers. I want to grasp onto them and tell him things will be okay. But I know it wouldn't do any good because I have no damn clue what's going to happen to us, to this fucked up town.

"As some of you may know, beloved citizens have come down with a strange illness. Unfortunately, the few doctors at the clinic can't seem to find out why that is. Their grave concerns for everyone's safety have encouraged me to call in the CDC. They've agreed to come down and take a look at the few of those who remain dangerously sick in the clinic. Now, please don't panic. I'm sure the doctors on their way will figure this out and do something in no time at all. We must have faith in God, in our people, and in the medical systems of this country!" I don't expect most of the crowd to jump from their seats in fits of joy.

And yet most of the older adults and elderly raise to their feet and shove their hands in the air.

I hurry to clasp my hands over my ears to shield their praise for the mayor. Their words of certainty and premature relief dig their way into my eardrums and try to push through my chest. This doesn't make me feel any better about this.

However, it's just me and my friends who remain sitting. The look on Crista's face is actually priceless. She definitely finds her mother's enthusiasm hilarious. I don't blame her.

My dad stands beside me with a wide strained smile. His

bright eyes linger on the mayor who waves his hands in the air, inhaling the words of thanks from the people of this town. To be honest, I have no idea if he believes in what he said.

Mayor Sparks isn't exactly the model resident of this place. On more than one occasion he's been spotted at titty bars in the next town over just west of us.

Yeah, I call bullshit on all of this.

Thomas shakes his head, laughing at the way his mom pretty much cries.

What the fuck is wrong with these people? I know most of us are freaks but this is some crazy shit.

I get why Bucky sneers at his dad to sit down and act right. It's embarrassing to watch all of these people simply believe in this. Don't they get that people have died over this awful sickness? All of us should panic and demand this to be fixed before it gets worse.

I have a bad feeling about all of this. It lingers in my guts like two-day-old pizza. We're so damn fucked and it's not even worth hysterically cackling over either.

8. Doctor, Doctor, Doctor

"These docs are one big juicy joke. Already, I've seen a few of them turn their noses up at us. How much help are they gonna be?" Thomas sputters through a mouth full of pizza.

Crista laughs so hard that she accidentally snorts her Coke into her nose.

I cringe as the dark bubbly beverage trails down her chin

and into her lap in the back of the Impala. She better not get that shit on my seats.

"Gross," I mumble. My fingers dig beneath the soft fur of Copper who sits between me and Bucky. I swear his nose twitches every time one of us opens the pizza box. I've given him all of my pepperoni from each slice of meat lovers I ate. How dare he drool for more?

Thomas takes a thick swallow before roughly coughing down his own threatening fits of giggles.

"Aren't there supposed to be more of them coming? There's only three down at the clinic." Bucky questions in the passenger seat next to me.

My eyes are temporarily glued to the brown and blonde curly strands of his hair shining in the light from the large glowing Pizza Hut sign that lingers tall. The reflection from the window strikes into his gaze that's directed at our other friends who are now currently arguing over the idea of stuffed crust.

To be fair, it's not a terrible one. But I'm not sure if that would be too much cheese. I can practically feel the stomach ache from that.

I'm glad they're engaging in talk about other not-so-important things. These past few days have been odd and unsettling. More families have fled Elora Falls and not to go on a typical summer vacation. Most had their cars and trucks full of their things. I doubt they will ever come back. Maybe they are the lucky ones.

After that meeting in April Square, people were left with conflicted feelings about the safety of this town. I don't think any of us can blame them for it. But I can't figure out if I should have let my dad take us away too. I would have found a way to convince my friends and their families to follow behind us too.

When we got home later that night he brought that possibility to the surface of all my dire questions. I said that we would be fine and that the CDC are more than capable of fixing things.

I fucking hope that I'm right about it because right now I have such little hope that's practically nonexistent.

Crista wipes off the sides of her mouth with a tan napkin. The pizza grease on her face quickly stains the paper. "I'm sure more reinforcements are on their way."

More boisterous cackles follow after her soft tone. Tears prick at my eyes and my insides threaten to squeeze the life out of me. Leave it to Crista to be the cautious one of us filled with innocence. Despite her sometimes bold stances, she is the softy of Shocker Pictures.

I tend to find myself wondering how the hell she tamed Thomas. It's a miracle that he stopped spray painting the town's only billboard of the school's mascot. I'm more than certain it was Crista who chewed his ass out for it.

Bucky looks like he's about to spill more hilarious words from that precious brain of his when the ground beneath the car starts to rumble. His jaw drops open in shock.

I grip the steering wheel in fright. Copper growls lowly next to me, his ears pinned to his head as a warning. I wonder how he didn't hear it sooner.

The others complain about the sudden earthquake. Their curious suggestions fail to properly reach me as I notice four massive army vehicles roll down the road right in front of us. My eyes widen at the troubling sight. Then a literal tank follows behind a line of medical trucks that has got to be hosting doctors, nurses, and their supplies. Damn, that is a lot of people compared to the normal outsiders we get per year. I've got a bad feeling about this. Well, I have a bad feeling about everything.

"Oh, shit." I peer into the rearview mirror at Crista's rapidly paling face.

Thomas takes her hand and gives it a reassuring clench. The motion encourages me to scratch behind Copper's ear before switching the key. The engine grumbles as I quickly rush into the street behind this terrifying military convoy.

Is it a good idea? Hell no.

"Char, keep a distance," Bucky utters softly. I notice his hand resting on the seat as close as possible to my thigh. He doesn't regard Copper at all. I almost imagine that he wishes to touch me for a little ounce of comfort. Yet I know it's just where he managed to place his hand. There is nothing serious to consider about it.

I give him a huff in answer. The slight smirk he does gives butterflies in my belly more enthusiasm to flutter madly. Damnit.

Without thinking I take a sharp right at the next street, evading the bright red light that signals stop. Hell, the sheriff can rest me later. It wouldn't be the first time I was stopped for speeding or running a red light. I've got a feeling it won't be the last either. I have a collection of those little yellow papers back at home hidden under my bed to spare my dad some embarrassment.

If he ever found out about them he'd have a fit. I rather him not see how much of a trouble I've become over the years. Just because I get in these situations doesn't mean I want to flaunt it like some people. That includes Jake and Thomas. Both want everyone to know their crazed chaos.

By almost doubling the car speed we beat the army guys to April Square. As soon as I spotted their ugly bland green vehicles I knew they would head for the only place in town where all of us meet up.

I barely park the car when all of us jump out with quick feet. After quickly clasping his leash onto his collar, I guide Copper behind me. I grunt due to his odd jittering form.

He keeps his growling to a whisper, and for that I'm glad. He has a habit of being rude to new people or outsiders who accidentally wander into town when I take him out for his weekly street walk. But it's a good thing that almost everyone in Elora Falls is familiar with him. Or else I fear he'd rip someone apart very viciously.

He's not mean. Copper is like my guardian in a way. I love him for that.

Those who have been hanging around in April Square spot us. Their small kids send my loyal companion very enthusiastic waves. I send most of them an exaggerated wink, a little promise that we'll come around later after all this chaos is over so that they can give Copper some attention. He loves the attention more than any dog I've ever seen.

He's even got his own bed at the post office for when he goes with Dad to work some mornings.

"What the fuck are these punks gonna do?" Old Man Cal shouts. His long silver beard flickers with his words. Damn, when was the last time he washed that camo cap of his? I can smell the sour stench from here.

Another man next to him, Jonhney, scoffs. "Why don't you just keep yer mouth shut and then maybe we'll know."

A few mutters of agreement seep into the air. Others shake

their head in question.

I roll my eyes. There will always be those who can't keep their mouths shut.

Me and my friends stop in the center of the square. All the chairs from our last meeting have been moved out of the way and stacked onto the stage. Perhaps to give the CDC more room for their operation. The thought doesn't make me feel any more relieved that they're here at all.

I'm beginning to hate what our little town is becoming in such a short amount of time.

The first military vehicle opens up and a very pristine woman wearing a crisp white lab coat with tall black heels climbs down. Despite the fancy shoes that don't belong here she gets out with simple ease.

Her long black hair sweeps over her shoulder with each powerful step she takes toward us. I wonder what conditioner she uses because there is no possibility of frizz.

I swallow thickly as her sharp green eyes pick at us, dissecting every part of what we are. She's probably used to high-tech facilities and fresh warm tea. Too bad she won't be finding any of that here. Almost all of us are built on hot steaming coffee with no cream or sugar.

That eerie grin of hers causes my stomach to flip. Crista taps her foot in a nervous sputter. I see Thomas give an irritated glare. Bucky of course offers a friendly smile as the people start to spill out of the convoy. I'm surprised he hasn't acquired a welcome bouquet of bright red roses.

When the lady opens her mouth an angry wave of red clouds covers my vision.

"Hello, people of Elora Falls. We have heard of your peculiar sickness and have come to remedy it to the best of our abilities.

79

Please, don't be alarmed. A system to ensure our safety we'll soon be set in place. I, Dr. Avery, will make sure to make you all comfortable. Now, I highly advise everyone to go home for the night and listen to the news station for any additional information."

Her speech sounds fair and solid. And yet all I can feel is disbelief. Sure, it's a rehearsed chain of words, but that doesn't mean it's true. Did she practice this on the way here? I'd bet ten bucks she did.

From the look of Crista's heavy side-eye, I know she can sense the same thing. At least I'm not the only one.

A few other older folks give their cautious protest. The sheriff and his deputy shuts them down and order all of us to return home and away from others. He and his cops usher the town folk back to their cars and bikes.

My movements are filled with hesitation. I can't explain why I'm so apprehensive about this. They're here to help those who are sick and prevent any more cases from happening. Maybe it's that movie knowledge that I have a bad habit of applying to real everyday life.

Despite my worry, I must have faith in whatever system they have planned for us that they truly mean to give aid and not screw us over.

Here we are again, lingering inside the car in front of Bucky's house.

The minute I drove us away from April Square, a thick gray fog had slipped over the town. It now acts like a hideous cover, trapping the high moon, and making our surroundings darker.

I took the rest of my friends home before the deep rumbles in the clouds began. Now it's just me and Bucky and my dear Copper. The dog slouches in the backseat. His various coos keep my mind focused. It's like he keeps reminding me that he is here with me and doesn't plan on going anywhere. I wonder if he knows I'm upset about my friends leaving at the end of the month.

"Look, I get that you're concerned about this whole CDC thing. But maybe we should keep our rather strong opinions to ourselves in case they truly mean to help." Bucky gives me a pointed look, his eyebrows raising too. Gosh, he sounds so proper. There is no ounce of a musty football player in his tone. I hate when he tries to make sense of things. he should go back on the field and throw a ball or two before telling me what's best to do.

It calls for all of my willpower not to scoff at him.

81

"Okay, fine. I'll keep my mouth shut until I find something fishy." I shake my head in anger.

Bucky huffs and turns away from me, gazing out of the window at his house. The pale yellow porch light shines into the car. It's a mediocrity of brightness. I wonder when his father last changed the bulb. Its occasional flicker lets me know it was a while ago.

"Please, don't go fishing for anything dangerous," Bucky says in a low tone that makes my heart skip two beats.

He's asking me to not be me. I'm not sure if that's possible.

I bite the inside of my cheek as he leans over to grip my shoulder. His touch causes my skin to engulf in invisible flames. I feel all icky on the inside every time we lock eyes. How can he do this to me without even knowing it?

I say nothing more. Bucky gives a heavy sigh before getting out of the Impala. Before closing the door he turns around and opens his mouth as if he wants to speak. But he thinks better of it and gives me a wink instead.

A small smirk grows on my face as I watch him literally skip to the front door, his beautiful curls swaying over his shoulders.

However, a strange cough behind me interrupts the many fantasies that try to infiltrate my mind.

With a jerk of my body, I'm completely facing the back seat. I see Copper lying down, his eyes more droopy than normal. He's probably tired from being out all day and so far away from his luscious bed. I know the feeling.

I attempt to reach my arm over to him, wanting to gently caress his dark blonde and black fur. His odd growl stops me from doing so. That's certainly new.

My brows raise in surprise. "Alright. We're going home,

Cop."

This seems to brighten his mood. His nose does that little satisfied twitch as I turn the engine on again. Sometimes I can feel that he understands literally everything I say.

Occasionally, I peek into the rearview mirror to make sure he's okay. I'm not totally convinced that he feels good when he trudges into the house behind me and plops into his bed. Maybe he had too much pizza today. Again, I know the feeling.

9. Runaway Doggo

Before my head hit the pillow last night I wanted to call the vet as soon as the early morning sun rose high in the sky. I didn't want to wait until Copper got sicker to do so.

However, when I do manage to get myself out of bed, dressed in a loose band shirt, and checkered pj pants, I discover that the landline phone doesn't work. I click a few buttons but nothing seems to make that dead ringing sound go away.

With an aggravated huff, my ruffled bangs flutter against my forehead.

"Huh." We've never had a problem with this phone and I'm pretty sure my dad paid the electrical company last week. This is odd and I don't like it. Well, maybe it's just that paranoid feeling I always seem to have trying to claw out of me.

I hang the phone back up and walk away with a strong yawn. I'll have to find a payphone somewhere in town later today if he gets worse.

Speaking of Copper, he hasn't moved from his bed at all in the night. I find him in front of the fireplace in the living room. His large bed sits on the dark brown carpet right before the red bricks.

"Hey, Cop." I keep my voice soft as I crisscross my legs to sit next to him.

His big body is shivering. My face scrunches due to my sudden confusion. It's around eighty degrees outside and almost seventy-five inside the house. If anything he should be sweating, that is if dogs could actually sweat. However, he is panting madly. I feel awful for him.

He still has that cough from last night too. Only it sounds more rough and wet. It could be a lung infection or something. I'm not an expert on dogs so I have no fucking clue. My best guess is it's due to the weird rhythm of rain we've been getting here. But that doesn't make sense since this is typical Elora Falls weather and he's lived here his entire life.

In truth, Copper's immune system should be more robust than this.

Poor guy must be really sick. Perhaps it's like when people get like that too. He could use some fresh air even if it's all hot

85

and slightly moist. Yeah, that's a good idea for sure.

"C'mon, Copper. Let's get ya outside." I usher him out of bed. His sluggish body limps all the way to the back door in such slow motion I think I might fall asleep like this.

He attempts to use the doggy door, but he's too weak to move the flap. With a deep frown, I unlock the whole door and gently pull it open.

Copper doesn't wait for me to walk him out further down the porch steps and into the forest. His tired feet carry him further until I watch him disappear into the thick trees. He'll come back once he feels better. He always does.

I turn to head back into the house, only to stop abruptly at the sight of a bright yellow paper that's been taped to the door.

My body shivers as I look around. There isn't anyone but me here. My dad left for work hours ago. Yeah, this is creepy.

"Freak," I growl as if somehow the person who plastered it on the door can hear me.

I rip it off, some of the top tearing in the process.

The paper is heavy in my slightly trembling hands. A logo of the CDC is printed at the top or should have been if I hadn't torn it.

It reads very clearly:

Dear citizens of Elora Falls,

Don't be alarmed by this safety warning. A system has been put in place to ensure your health. Keep to these simple rules while CDC personnel fight this new illness so no one else gets sick.

- *Avoid the forest that surrounds Elora Falls*
- *Avoid toads and mushrooms if possible*
- *Refuse contact with anyone who sports a fever*

Thank you for your cooperation.
  Dr. Avery of the CDC

"Why the fuck do we need to avoid toads?" I ask out loud after slamming the door behind me once I'm back inside the house.

This doesn't make any sense.

An itch to crumble the paper sings in my fingers. I place it on the kitchen counter before heading upstairs to change into a random pair of jeans I find on the floor. I keep on the shirt I wore last night to bed.

After roughing up my hair and adjusting my bangs I head back down. Once I fetch the key to the car I'm out of the front door in a flash on my way to the school for the final pre-rehearsal before we host local auditions for the lead.

I can't believe we didn't even get to mess around with a few scenes before that asshole kicked us out. Does he know that we got permission from the theater program and the principal to film in the auditorium? I guess not because the new teacher stormed inside with a face so red I was afraid he would explode.

What a fucking loser! I'll be damned if he runs us out of the school next time. He's lucky I didn't toss my director chair at his balding head that's covered in wispy red strands coated in summer sweat

"Char, you look like you're gonna pop." Thomas leans over the seat to peer at me.

I give him a rightful snarl.

He backs off with a grin and his hands are held up in surrender.

Crista shakes her head. I see her wet hair plastered to her face. My skin crawls with my own hair that clings to my flesh like a second skin. The golden tendrils wrapping around my forehead and neck like the fingers of death gripping its next victim. Well, that's a little dramatic but that's what the ugly sensation feels like.

It started raining the moment we left the school. Large drops clash against the hood of my car as we stroll down the streets of Elora Falls. The thumping sounds almost drown out the song 'Danger Zone' by Kenny Loggins. I can barely hear the catchy lyrics.

We are technically breaking the rules by hanging out together. A good point that the new teacher made as he shoved us out the front doors with angry fists waving in the heated air. But none of us have a fever and we haven't seen any mushrooms or toads. I'm still not even sure what they have to do with all the sick people in this town.

As my friends converse about the paper that's been stuck to every window and door those doctors could find, I start to twist the car down lanes and avenues that ultimately lead down to my road. I surprisingly don't know all the street names but

I do know the way through this town. I can get myself around the various bakeries and boring playgrounds that the small children of this town frequent.

No one seems to notice me approach my driveway.

Crista shushes Thomas by whacking the back of his head. Bucky snorts into his hands. All of them go quiet when they peer out the windshield and see the two-story house I sometimes struggle to call home. The pillars of the massive porch are gloomy in the darkness that is consumed with this heated rain.

"Y-You brought us to your place? Are you sure you aren't coming down with something?" Crista leans close and grasps the edge of the seat.

"I'm pretty sure I'm drenched in rain, not sweat." I bite back a grin.

Thomas chuckles to himself before getting out. The down-pour of rain instantly seeps into his hair, sliding off his leather jacket like black oil.

"Well, good enough for me." I watch Crista through the side mirror as she adjusts her ruined blue fuzzy sweater before hopping out as well.

Bucky follows shortly. I'm not sure why I feel guilty that his nice letterman is getting all wet. I shouldn't since it's all he wears. We have that in common. It's what sets us apart from the rest of the friend gangs that are in this town. There is something about it that makes us, well... Us. Shocker Pictures.

And yet somehow he is more gorgeous than ever standing in the blinding porch light. I take a few seconds to admire his solid cheekbones and full lips.

When he shoots me a curious look I hurry out of the car. All of us rush up the steps. Our breaths are rugged from the speed of our movements and adrenaline coursing through our veins.

No matter how different we are or what individual things we enjoy, we are so much alike. It's awesome in my opinion. And that's why it will break my heart when all three of them leave me here.

"Dad?" I call out into the foyer when I get the front door unlocked.

My voice echoes up the stairs and throughout the kitchen.

"No one's home." Thomas sounds elated at that fact.

I hear Crista hit his shoulder before both of them find their way to the couch in the living room. I'm sure they'll be snooping around soon.

None of my friends have been here. I never found a reason for them to come far out of their way. Plus, Crista's parents never seem to have a problem with it.

But maybe they should see my so-called safe place at least once.

I ignore the fluttering feelings I get when seeing their eyes examine where I dwell when I'm not with them. It's odd.

"Wow." Bucky gasps lightly to my right.

I carefully twist around to see his striking hazel eyes peer all around him. They twinkle with curiosity. He takes in the weird pieces of art my dad likes to collect from random yard sales. They're his favorite things to decorate with. Since my mother passed he wanted to take down everything that reminded us of her. Then he replaced them with these funky paintings. I never questioned him for it. It's what he needed to heal.

And I don't mind their strangeness. They pair well with this wonderfully cozy house.

"You like?" I ask, taking a few steps forward with my arms

raised in a presenting motion.

He nods eagerly, clearly infatuated with his surroundings. I could have never guessed that my house would be worth drooling over. I guess all the suspense led to something great.

Hmm, I could make a movie out of that premise. All I would need is maybe some scene cards and—

"Hey, I found Copper's fucking big ass bed, but he's not in it," Crista calls out from the living room.

My brows furrow. "What do you mean he isn't there?"

A nervous chuckle echoes.

"Well, Ms. Sherlock, the bed is empty and Copper is missing." Thomas sounds amused but it's paired with a slightly worried tone.

Huh? That is strange. No matter what, Copper always greets me at the door. I should have realized something was wrong as soon as I reached the porch and didn't hear any excited woofs.

Bucky follows me as I casually shuffle into the living room. My heart is racing too high.

My eyes widen at the empty dog bed. I lean down and let my fingers brush against the soft inside. Its cozy fluff is cold and has long been abandoned.

"He hasn't been here for a while. I let him out early this morning. I guess he just went out again and hasn't heard us yet." That's not what I'm really thinking.

Crista fiddles with her hands as I stand. Her face pulled with unnatural tension. She'll get wrinkles if she keeps frowning.

Bucky's brow arches in question. "That's not normal for him."

My heart skips a few beats at how much this guy actually notices things about me. Too bad I'm worried about my suddenly missing dog.

"You guys stay here. I'm going to find Copper." My red coat crinkles as I make my way to the back door.

A throat clearing behind me stalls my movements. With a roll of my eyes, I twist around with a slight smile. I knew they wouldn't just sit and wait till I got back. Where is the sense in that? They must want the adventure too.

The three of them stand there. Crista has her hands on her hips, giving me a pointed look. Thomas rubbing his hands together like an evil movie villain. And then there's Bucky, offering me a simple expression.

"Fine. If you're going with me I must confess to something." Now they really look worried.

After a few moments of silence, I present an idea that I've been mulling over for a while. It's an extremely idiotic and potentially dangerous idea. They all have to want in on it. There will be no going back.

"We should scrap the movie and make a documentary." Their annoyed groans fuel my own mocking ones.

"Please don't tell us you want the documentary to be about whatever the fuck is happening in Elora Falls." Thomas shakes his head, a wild grin that singles a 'yes' sitting on his lips. He whips his dark hair back as his body convulses in silence fits of giggles.

I knew he'd enjoy this. But what about the others?

"You've had some interesting ideas in the past, but this is totally in a different ballpark. However, you might be onto something. If you think this will look good on our resumes then I'm in." Crista crosses her arms and gives me a firm nod.

Yes. I knew she would eventually see my vision. Most of the time she makes me explain all of my thoughts before she even considers helping me. She is very thorough that way. This could either make or break us. I'm glad she's willing to take the risk like I am.

I turn to Bucky. He thinks for a moment. Most likely considering the pros and cons of this. I get it. This could be dangerous. Deadly.

"I'm with you no matter what." Now that is the answer I was looking for.

A smile engulfs my face. My cheeks are on fire from the excitement that rushes through my spine. This is going to be totally awesome.

I clear my throat, standing a little straighter. "Get the camera. We've got a missing dog to find and a mystery to uncover."

10. Copper

Surprisingly chilly rain pours over us as we venture deeper into the town's forest. My feet squish in the sour mud, making a squelching noise—the sound scratches against my eardrums too bizarrely.

I lead the way through the tall looming cedar and fragrant pine trees with Shocker Pictures trailing behind me. Their harsh breathing from all this unusual exercise is a slight comfort.

After a while, I stop us and give firm instructions on how I want this to pan out. None argue with me. I'm not sure if I want them to or not. Anything would be better than them not fighting against me at all. Where is the struggle that they usually bring me? I'll be waiting for it to come later.

Crista takes charge and gives Bucky pointers about addressing an audience even when they really aren't there. Her words are precise and well presented and he fully understands with little question. Thomas angles the camera to peer at him, letting it sit on his leather-covered shoulder to catch Bucky's best side profile. I helped him adjust it a bit before I was happy with it.

We continue marching forth—the wet seeps into my hair, plastering it to my forehead. I'm grateful to always have my red coat with me. It does get rough when the rain takes over this place. I sort of despise the hair on my arms standing up straight from the chill the weather usually brings.

"My name's Bucky Sinclair and I'm an 88' Elora Falls High School graduate. Just two months after I and my classmates walked across the stage a strange illness decided to roll into the town of Elora Falls, a nice little place here in Oregon that is always covered in rain." Bucky speaks into the camera with such ease.

It reminds me of the many times the local news station did small interviews with him after his games to air on the TV. I'd watch them after coming home hours later to admire his uniformed posture despite spending a few hours running around on the field.

He's not a real shy person so this is a walk in the park for him. I'm sure he's flattered by the attention.

He struts backward, occasionally watching out for trees. I keep a good pace next to Thomas. I make sure to fix any odd angles that sneak around. My eyes are focused on the viewer part of the camera.

Crista gives Bucky advice about facial expressions and having a genuine connection with the camera. I think it's due to the way she always envisioned a documentary. A few years ago she mentioned wanting to film one of her own someday. Well, it's a good thing we are doing one right now about something so awful.

I keep my mouth shut despite me being the director. It's not just about what I want. This is an important project for all of us, a last chance to be with each other before everything gets worse. I don't want it to end, ever.

"Alright, you can cut for a while. At least until we find anything worth filming." I give a slight order, keeping my voice a little higher as the rain pelts against the tree canopy.

My bones are cold. It takes great effort to safely step over large rocks and broken logs that are covered in sweet green moss.

Our flashlights of various shades of yellow light cast unique shadows before us. Dark shapes blend in with the gloomy forest floor. I can see the many drops of rain sink into the moist dirt, clinging to the roots of plants, and gathering for the worms and grubs that dwell beneath our feet.

But the more I study everything the more confused I become. I've yet to see any red-capped mushrooms. Instead, there are so many tall thin ones that almost seem to glow an odd shade of green.

"Wait." My shout is so quiet that I can barely hear it myself. Our footsteps stall abruptly.

"W-What is it?" Crista asks through her chattering teeth.

"Point the lights and camera to the ground. Look at this shit." It's not excitement that lingers in my tone. I'm afraid it's fear.

"What do you want me to say, boss?" I fail to find Bucky's funny nickname pleasing.

I clear my throat. "The paper the CDC put on all our doors said to avoid mushrooms and toads. I think this is what they meant. Talk about that."

He nods his head and does exactly as I ask. Bucky crouches close to the ground, but not too close to touch the many fungi that glow a wicked green.

My chest aches as his soaked curls glide over his shoulders. A few stands coil around his ears, I wish his ears were my freezing fingers. I shake the quick vivid idea out of my head before glancing around after he finishes up.

I have to say that he's a natural at this. I wonder what major he'll choose once he goes off to school.

One day he could possibly be a sports reporter. Yeah, he'd be killer at it.

"Hey! Look at that." Thomas breaks through my thoughts with his suddenly shrill voice.

We all look around for a moment till we spot what the camera is pointing at.

"Shit," I mumble as a white toad hops forward.

My stomach recoils inside me at the sight of those strange mushrooms that seem to be growing out of its large back. Gosh, this thing is fucking huge. Almost as big as my dog. I really don't want to find out why Dr. Avery and the rest of the military people want us to keep away from this hideous amphibian.

Before I can truly register what I'm seeing, Thomas shoves

the still-rolling camera into Bucky's hands and gets on his knees before the toad, his eyes wide with pure curiosity that has no room for fright.

"What the fuck are you doing?" Crista hisses at him, clutching her bag to her chest tightly.

"Man, this is stupid." Bucky shakes his head.

No words form in my mouth. I have no idea what to say. This is a bad idea. Thomas knows it too.

"My name is Thomas Jones and this is one big fucking frog." He exclaims right into the camera, pulling it forward with Bucky attached to it still.

"Toad." Crista corrects him.

I bit my lip hard due to this sickening harsh anticipation.

What am I doing? Why am I suddenly speechless? Fuck this.

"Thomas, I'm only going to say this once. Back off or else I'll kick you so far up your ass that you fly out of this fucking forest." I'm glad that I no longer feel numb.

His grand smile slips into a frown, then it morphs into a sneer.

"Jeez, Char. Do you ever lighten up? I'm just having some fun in this boring ass town. Is that a crime now too?" He spits at me before gripping the traveling toad in his large shaky hands. It does its best to squirm.

"No! What the hell are you doing?" A cry shoots out from Crista.

"You're crazy!" Bucky declares as Thomas begins to swing around the disgusting creature who has bright yellow eyes, like a cat. Oh, the poor thing flails madly to escape and jet my friend only grips it tighter in response. I think he's choking it!

"Fucking moron." I move to get that thing out of his grasp. But he jerks back so hard away from me that he clenches it too tightly.

A wet gushing sound stills me. Mounds of transparent yellow goop ooze out of the pores that the mushrooms sprout from, leaking all over his hands and fingers. The smell of rot causes me to gag. I back up a few paces so that he can toss the massive toad onto the ground.

It lands in a pile of fallen leaves with a sickening thud. I flinch from the small croak it manages to make. I don't get the chance to watch it hobble along to its business when Thomas starts to freak you.

His disgusted shouts fill the forest. Thomas scrubs his hands onto his pants. He even finds the nearest puddle, falls onto his stomach, and hurriedly wipes his fingers clean.

All of our movements come to a stop. My breaths move in and out of me in quick spurts. Is this hyperventilating?

A low growling vibrates my spine. I know that sound. In a slow unison, those of us left standing follow our flashlights to the disturbing noise.

Before I gasp I clamp my mouth shut. Tears brought on by anger and confusion leak down my face, milling with the faint rain. I hadn't noticed it letting up.

"Oh, Copper." Bucky sighs in defeat.

The dog in question, the little beast we've been looking for, stands crooked in front of Thomas.

He slowly moves back to his feet, bracing himself before Crista. Despite being an asshole who enjoys sparking trouble, he will always do everything in his power to keep her safe. I guess he can be a softy after all. Why couldn't he act right earlier instead of performing as a child? We will never find the answer to that.

"Hey, Cop. I know you don't feel too good, bud." My

words shake at the sight of my dog, my best friend who sways dangerously quick.

Most of his pretty multicolored fur is missing. His once pink skin now holds this pale yellow tint. Those round eyes of his have got this green shade that shrouds over them. Various-sized wounds cover his frail body. They leak a foul green sludge that smells horrendous. How did he drop weight so fast? This is crazy.

His growling engulfs the forest and our silence along with it. My soul aches, begging to take his pain away. How did I not notice the signs of this earlier? I had been too busy trying to unveil this fucking conspiracy.

"It's okay. I'm here." I know at the surface of my heart that Copper isn't really in his right mind. He has no idea who I am or my friends. He was gone the moment I let him wander out into the trees. I should have been there before the lights went out in his dogly sanity.

And just like that, anger rushes into my chest like a battering ram used to take over someone's magical castle.

"Charlie, it's not him anymore." Bucky's wonderful voice fails to convince me to back away from him.

I take two steps forward. Copper howls into the air when my foot accidentally snaps a twig. More tears stream down, mixing with my snot, and falling off my chin.

"Copper?" His brutal wails of pain strike me deeply. The high-pitched screams are so unnatural for him. A dog shouldn't be able to make such noise.

Thanks to the light blasting from flashlights around us I see something wriggle underneath his severely damaged skin. It takes little time to move so vigorously that my dog topples over, his leaking snout touching the edge of the muddy puddle.

"Please." I'm not sure who or what I'm pleading to. I don't believe in any god. Never have and especially not since the passing of my mother. But I never wanted to badly do so before now. Where will his little soul, if he has one, go once he dies? The endless possibilities only fuel my sobs.

I feel someone grip my coat behind me. I don't know who it is nor do I care.

"No!" I shout as Copper jerks around, his frail body convulses so badly that pieces of him are slipping off of his bones.

More of that spoiled smell consumes my senses. This time vomit makes its way out of my throat. I bend over to evacuate my stomach.

After watching my dog melt in front of me into a pile of sickening green mush, I think I can finally breathe.

But my heartfelt cries make it hard to breathe at all.

I know that it is Bucky who wraps his arms around me. His hair that I so dearly love twines with mine. It's not enough to break me out of this endless cycle of torment. Never did I think I'd lose someone else that I love. This can't be happening. I'm locked in a nightmare with no room for fucking escape. So this is what movie heroes feel like when the villain has finally outsmarted them.

"What the fuck is that?" Thomas squeaks.

I wipe my face to clear my vision.

Whatever is left of my Copper seems to pulsate. The fungi on the forest floor and toad sprout from the pile in majestic waves. Their glow illuminates the dark soil around them. They wiggle around each other, almost like there is a familiar sense in the air that none of us can feel.

Shockingly, the pile of green mush moves away from us at

101

an alarming rate.

That's all it takes for me to lose my shit and shout till my throat grows hoarse.

Act II

ACT
II

THE MUSH

11. What Do We Do Now?

My feet ache as I step onto the porch at a slow pace. After all that I've seen tonight, I think I deserve not to rush into anything. Now that's a first for me.

The rain let up for a while. Long enough for us not to sink into the mud as we trudged back through the thick trees in a stammering motion.

Warm air hits me in the face, instantly drying my tears as I limp into the foyer with my friends close behind me. My body is so drained that I collapse the moment my legs hit the couch.

With lazy eyes, I watch Thomas sprint to the kitchen behind me. The water from the faucet spills rapidly and many pumps from the soap spout sound off. I bet he's using the dishware scrubber to clean his entire body. Jeez, any rougher and his skin will be peeling off his hands.

Crista sits on the coffee table with her knees pinned together tightly. Her red bleary eyes are dead set on the cold empty bed that used to be Copper's.

Oh, my poor Copper. Thinking about how much he suffered brings me into soft fits of tears. Every part of me trembles. Bucky sinks into the cushion next to me, his arm snaking around me.

I sob hard into his shoulder. My salty tears soak his letterman but neither of us gives a damn. I want this nightmare to end already and then when I wake my dog will be in his bed sleeping soundlessly.

"This shit isn't natural," Crista says calmly.

"No fucking shit!" Thomas shouts, making me jump in fright.

Bucky shushes them both. All that lingers in the air is the tension brought on by this new revelation.

Not wanting to dwell in my pain, I rip away from his hold and get on my feet. A shaking sigh flees past my lips. I trail my fingers through my hair, pushing the unruly gold strands behind my ears. My mind is consumed with instant thoughts of this thing's origins.

I clear my throat. "Whatever the fuck this sickness is, someone made it."

105

There is no doubt about that. Nature might be one helluva bitch, but there is no way this came about like it's nothing. I won't believe that for a damn second.

No wonder the CDC came so quickly. They better have a way to fix it before it gets worse and more people start to turn up missing. Or else they will get a face full of my fist. And they should be careful because I know how to use it.

"I guess it doesn't matter who or what did it. The docs want to cover it up. We should let them and be done with this shit." Bucky shrugs his shoulders.

"As long as that doesn't involve wiping out the whole town then we should be good, right? Right?" Thomas almost sounds convinced. But he has the best-unspoken point that I'm sure Bucky didn't want to openly question.

He struts out from behind the couch with a wet kitchen towel in his hands, wiping every part of his skin dry still. He's making an utter mess as he accidentally slings water drops everywhere.

"Go take a damn shower. Use my dad's clothes." I tell him before he gets the chance to strip down in front of us to clean his other dirty bits.

"T-That only happens in the movies," I mutter to him as he skips up the stairs with Cirsta hurrying to follow behind him.

With a harsh cry, I say, "No funny business up there. This is my house!"

I hear a nervous giggle after a door is slammed. That bastard probably chose my bathroom to use. I'll get him for that. As soon as I find the strength to feel real anger.

In agitated movements, I take Crista's seat. Copper's bed looks so empty. I can't believe what the fuck I saw. It doesn't seem real.

That's what happened to Amy and Peter?

I don't realize I spoke those words out loud until Bucky answers me. "At least they went quick if it did happen like that."

I give him a snort. He responds with a chuckle. Nothing in me finds either of them amusing.

Silence drifts within the house. It weaves through me as I continue to stare at the basket of toys Copper used to drag along the carpet. A few of the stuffed animals are missing their plastic eyes. I wouldn't be surprised if he once chewed them off and ate them for a snack. That wouldn't have resulted in a hard time in taking his shits.

A smile threatens to grip my lips and tug them apart. But I refuse to allow it to happen.

The sadness that tries to force itself into my guts instantly dissipates when thumping footsteps tread back into the living room. Jeez, I must have been staring at the toys for at least thirty minutes. I don't ever space out like that. I squirm in disgust.

Both Thomas and Crista look nice and fresh. I doubt they listened to what I said earlier. But at least they seem fine. Well, except for him. His arms and neck are red from scrubbing too hard. I'm guessing as long as he didn't get any of that shit in his mouth he'll be okay. I really fucking hope so.

They fill the rest of the couch. All of them look at me with either pity or confusion clouding their eyes. I don't have it in me to figure out which it is.

I don't want their sadness. It will only make me angry. I'm already pissed that I couldn't do something, anything to ease his suffering.

Ignoring the stray tear that drips down my face I clear my

throat to interrupt this sadness.

"What do we do now?" Crista asks. Her tone is gentle.

The huff I give is filled with amusement.

"That's the question, isn't it? What do we do now? Well, I vote that we finish what we started." My throat aches from the sobs and cries I shed in the forest.

No one speaks for a while. They let my words simmer, sinking into their minds, and giving them a moment to figure out what they want to do. They're lucky I'm willing to listen to their thoughts about this at all and not be a dick about it.

Thomas scratches the back of his neck, avoiding my gaze. "So, you want to spy on these freak docs and uncover what the hell they did to our town? And to one day expose the truth to the public?"

I nod.

"Could you imagine what that could do for us? Hell, I could get a job anywhere with that on my resume. I vote yes." Crista says almost breathlessly.

She may be thinking about her future but I know she also wants people to know what's going on, whatever that may be. She's nice like that.

Bucky is the last to say something. I find that troubling. He gets off the couch and sits down next to me, his knee touches mine. I suppress a shiver.

"Okay, I'm in." That's all it takes for me to grip his knee in return. A soft expression consumes his features. Yes, no matter what I knew he would follow me.

I sniff deeply before getting up on my feet. I wipe my face again, hating the feel of dried tears on my already-flushed skin. Despite the cold rain that pelts on the roof I'm still a sweaty mess. All this annoyance and sudden grief have made me so heated.

"We all sleep here tonight. Call your parents so they won't send a search party for you guys later. We can't afford for those docs to get a whiff of what we're doing." None protest. That's more than good enough for me. I'm glad that the phone is working again.

Crista helps me find a few spare blankets in the foyer closet. We make a pallet with them in front of the couch after pushing the coffee table to the side. The guys fetch pillows from my room. I'm glad there isn't anything stashed in there that will embarrass me. I guarantee they took too long to do it so Thomas could snoop. What an asshole.

I don't bother to change into pajamas. I'm too tired.

Bucky takes the couch while Crista is sandwiched between me and Thomas. Her arms wrap around my shoulders in a comforting manner. I fail to accept the gentle touch. I'm a rigid plank made of solid defeat. I fear that nothing will feel comforting anymore. That the simple touch from someone I love who remains in my life will remain foreign and tragic. It won't get rid of this throbbing ache that rests in my heart.

I knew from the beginning things weren't right. They told me I was crazy and reaching too far into the unbelievable. Perhaps now they will see what I see. A hidden scheme that's right before our eyes.

And now that Copper is gone, I'm more convinced this might not have been an accident at all.

But maybe that's my paranoia talking. I always did think outside the box when it wasn't necessary. This will be my movie villain's downfall. Wouldn't that be one helluva ending? I think about the possibility as my exhaustion sinks me into sleep.

12. Fenced In

I t's a damn miracle that we manage to sneak inside the school without being noticed.

There are CDC personnel crawling around the town dressed in their bright pink hazmat suits, carrying transparent clipboards gripping neon green papers. Many have taken up shop in the cafeteria and gym of the school, using the space as medical setups for all their experiments to try to cure this sickness. If that's actually what they're doing, that is.

Good thing no one was occupying the auditorium. It gives us the perfect cover to prepare for our self-filmed interviews.

On the way here I came up with the idea to interview each of us. To talk about what we've seen so far and what we expect to happen. I'd like us to do this at least twice a week until all of this shit is over. Who knows if that will actually happen.

"Hey, what if we start with Thomas? I mean, he did find that fucking big toad the other night." Bucky looks through the script for the movie I decided to scrap for this documentary. I don't doubt that he'll miss the idea of it. Hell, even I know it was a horrible movie. I bet he'll thank me for it later when we're famous for solving this mystery.

I shrug as I picture this narrative. "He can't goof off about it."

A short chuckle sounds off behind me.

"Whatever gets the message across." Thomas ruffles his dark hair before occupying my director chair that I got Bucky to set up in the middle of the stage.

A while ago I helped Crista pick which lights would create the best atmosphere and where to adjust them. Now a gentle pink light cascades over her boyfriend, highlighting his oddly sharp cheekbones.

He messes around with the sleeve of his leather jacket before Crista places another random chair in front of him. A smile breaks across his face as she takes a seat, a piece of paper in hand with all the questions I came up with to ask.

She smoothes back her red hair and clears her throat.

Bucky holds the camera to his shoulder, pointing down a little to capture both of their faces. I notice he's cutting a part of Thomas's forehead off with the frame. I hold my breath as

111

I carefully tilt the camera for him. He says nothing as I do this, only glances at me with a sparkle in his eye.

"Action!" I can hear the sudden grin that sprouts on my lips. It feels so good to say that. I knew this would be a good idea. After this, we need to find a way into the photography room to start splicing all these clips together. And then I'll come up with the title for this film.

Crista starts the interview by introducing herself and Thomas. She gives a short synopsis of what's been going on in Elora Falls. He follows with our school lives and how we started this film journey. It's a nice touch if I'm being honest.

"Alright, Thomas. I'd like to ask my first question." Crista crosses her legs. The pale pink velvet skirt she wears flows around her ankles perfectly. It matches well with her chunky green sweater. I braided her thick hair down her back as well and fluffed her newly cut bangs which are much fuller now.

Thomas raises his brows at her casual movement. "Sure thing, Miss Crista Fisher."

I shake my head as her face becomes flushed.

"What a dork." Bucky laughs softly into my ear. His breath tickles my flesh a little too comfortably.

He snickers into the camera.

She shakes her head and addresses him again.

For a solid hour, things go well. I speak up to see if she can ask something more detailed. Both give me their input on what they'd like to say. Bucky gives suggestions about changing the angle of their chairs and I fix up their hair. If I didn't know any better I'd say this was a professional gig.

"C-Can we take a break? Put Bucky in the chair for a bit." Thomas asks after answering a fourth question.

I nod to Bucky. He turns off the camera and places it on the edge of the stage.

"What's up?" I cross my arms. My red coat sleeves glide against the skin-tight shirt I'm wearing underneath that's the color of dark sand.

A while ago he took off his jacket. Somehow he's been sweating without it. It's a good seventy-two degrees in here and not cooking hot like it is outside. The front of his white shirt is utterly soaked. Drops of sweat trail down the sides of his face. I even made sure to turn down the temperature of the auditorium to avoid this. There wasn't a need for us to look a mess in front of the camera. And besides we needed to chill for a bit anyway.

"You okay?" Crista places the back of her hand on his forehead. She rips it away with a wince flying off her tongue.

"He's burning up." Bucky takes the small towel out of his back pocket. Something he uses to clear his skin and eyes when he's on the field.

I watch him carefully wipe Thomas's face clean.

I take a step back from all of them. My eyes go wide as I realize why he looks so green in the flesh.

"He's got it. T-The Mush." My words are so silent I almost don't hear myself.

"What the fuck is the Mush? Oh, fuck me." Thomas barks in new agony. His questioning tone quickly turns into a sickening cough.

Crista tries to pat him on the back to relieve his strain. He jolts from her touch, hissing in true discomfort.

"Well, we've got to call it something. Copper literally became a pile of mush. So, I'm calling it the Mush." Saying it out loud does sound bizarre. But I've got nothing else to name it.

Thomas laughs again, this time puking up green sludge in

113

the process. I cringe as the dark color spills over the deep gray stage floor.

He doubles over in coughing fits. Bucky tries settling him back in the seat. Thomas fights against him, vomiting on Crista in the process.

"Shit!" She curses and wipes his mouth clean with her sweater sleeve.

"We need to get him to the clinic. Maybe one of our nurses can help." I'll be damned if we go to those CDC bitches first.

She nods hurriedly in agreement.

In a quick motion, me and Bucky wrap Thomas's arms around us. I grunt from the weight. He's a lot heavier than he looks.

A huff escapes me as we rush down the steps of the stage. Our feet move fast and yet somehow too slow. I feel Crista's worried presence behind us.

She checks the halls before we enter them, looking out for anyone who will send us to either the mayor or our parents. Neither of these is a good option.

I inhale deeply once we make it outside. The air is warm and fills my lungs like a hug. If it weren't for this terrible situation I'd enjoy this weather. It's nice that it isn't raining for once.

"C'mon," I mutter.

Gently, we lead a groaning Thomas to my car. Crista gets in the back with him. She instantly places his limp head on her lap. She too is covered in a sweaty sheen.

I say nothing as I get in the driver's seat. There isn't time to dwell on her own furious flush. Once I twist the key the engine shouts loud.

A few of the medical staff of the CDC rush outside when they hear the car. I flip them off with a frown before driving off and out of the school parking lot. The action doesn't make me feel any less panicky.

"Hold on, baby." Crista cries softly into his hair. I watch from the rearview mirror as she caresses his sunken cheek.

I'm not sure when he last opened his eyes. Most likely when we made it to the clinic only to find it completely overrun by the CDC. My heart sank when I realized that none of our people would be able to help without getting them involved. They're everywhere, consuming the streets, slowly eating away at our uniqueness.

Our best bet was to turn around and head for the next town over. They have a real hospital there with real doctors and not these obvious freaks. A fresh set of eyes may do Thomas some good.

I'm surprised no sirens are trailing after us as I speed down the street like a strong winter wind. I keep my expression firm as Thomas cries from the backseat.

Bucky does his best to tell stories to soothe him. Crista can only hold him with tears falling onto her soiled sweater.

I know this illness, the Mush, is going to get worse. I just never imagined one of my best friends would get it too. Why didn't I make him put that fucking toad down sooner? Maybe listening to the CDC wasn't such a waste of our energy after all. Too bad we didn't really choose to follow their rules.

This has to be my fault. I should have tried harder.

"Damnit, fucking go faster!" Crista shouts after he throws up onto the floorboard.

The smell of it is horrible. It's a rotting stench similar to what that toad and Copper smelled like. Oh, shit. Thomas is decaying from the inside out.

The realization hits me as I drive us off the main road, leading us straight to the only exit and entrance of the town.

I blink through angry tears, biting my bottom lip to hold in a shout filled with frustration.

However, I can't let myself crumble now. It's not what my friends need me to be strong for them.

My nerves get worse when I see something sporting through the trees. My eyes widen at the sight of a massive chain fence that surrounds the edge of Elora Falls. We're so fucking screwed with this.

"What the fuck did they do to us?" Crista shouts. Her words strike my heart, each with an intense force.

I stall the car to an abrupt stop at the start of the bridge that leads over the rushing river. From up here I can still hear the waves crash against the rocky banks. The noise offers no comfort.

"They caged us in here. Those fuckers don't want to help us! You were right, Char. We should have listened sooner. " Bucky growls next to me. His curly hair slips from the bun he made earlier, curling around his neck and ears.

I say nothing once catching sight of Jake and his fucking goons scoping the fence. At least he too sports bruises from our fight like I do. Though his lip isn't still in literal pieces like mine is. It still aches every time I speak. I must look ridiculous with these fucking bandaids holding it together still.

And yet the itching is a good sign of its healing. I don't even care about the scar I'll have forever.

"Stay here," I order them. I don't wait for their protest before getting out.

A few of the guys slap Jake on the back to get his attention as I stalk toward them. He stops his harsh shouting long enough to catch sight of me. I wave my bangs out of my face so he can see the black eye he gave me. I hope it was worth it for him.

"What the fuck do you want?" His voice sings to me in ways that make me want to tackle him again. Maybe this time I won't lose.

I cross my arms. "How long has this thing been here?"

He scoffs, turning away from me to glare at the fence that has to be at least twenty feet high. Large spikes grace the top, a silent warning to stay the hell away from it. Too bad that most of us in this place don't listen to orders. That's been clear from the start.

"A few days." He answers me, though sounding irritated by my standing there. Good. I hate him too.

I huff in acknowledgment. My eyes water the higher I peer at it. They must have thought all of this out the moment word was sent to them about the Mush.

"Fuck it." Jake strips his multicolored bomber jacket with too many aggravated noises.

His friends attempt to stop him. He shrugs them away, his frown holding strong.

117

"Dude!" A guy's name I don't remember tries gripping his shoulder. Jake twists around like a snake to sock him in the jaw.

I fail to find any words to protest as he sizes up the fence like a new face to peel off. This fucker is a fool. He better not do what I think he wants to do.

He pushes the sleeves of his black shirt to his elbows before slowly gripping the silver fence.

I cross my arms. My face scrunches as Jake carefully plugs his black Converse into the openings, hooking his fingers to hoist himself further up.

"He's fucking nuts!" Bucky shouts from the car. I turn around to nod in agreement.

I'd find this amusing if it were any other day. However, this probably isn't the time to mess around. I still hear Thomas's wails of pain from where I'm standing near the fence. We need to get him out of here.

Jake reaches the top, his hands holding onto the thick railing tightly. My heart thumps madly in my chest, waiting in this icky anticipation. I bit the inside of my cheek to keep my mind focused.

"I may hate your guts but this is some crazy ass shit, Jake. Get down from there. C'mon, be serious for once in your loser life!" I can't keep silent any longer. Watching him struggle to keep his grip is putting knots in my stomach. This isn't right. Even he should know that.

"Nah, I'm almost over the top." He shouts down at me.

I roll my eyes and say nothing more.

My lungs squeeze tight the moment Jake's foot slips on the top rail, flipping him over in such a rushed motion that he doesn't catch himself. His fingers barely touch the rail. I see something dark flash across his wide eyes. Bile lurches in my throat.

A cry seeps out of me as he falls forward, his back catching onto the nearest spike. Its sharp point pierces his shirt, plunging into the flesh of his back with little effort. The sound of the point of the spike scraping against his spine is terrifying. It sinks into my ears. My gaze captures the sight of his entire back skin being torn off in one jagged motion. His friends call out in distress. I hear Bucky shouting from the car, urging me to return so we can get the hell out of here.

This time I listen to his words.

I don't wait around to see Jake's body plop down on the other side of the fence and onto the bridge.

There's music blasting from the speakers as I shakily get inside the Impala. A song called 'I Want to Break Free' by Queen starts to play when my fingers grasp the stirring wheel and gear shift.

It's an ironic choice of words to hear while driving away at full speed from a fucking fence that's keeping the entire town inside. There is no escape for us. More than likely we will all catch the Mush like Thomas and just fucking die. Maybe that's why the CDC did this. Because they know none of us will make it out alive and we're so damn screwed.

13. Goodbye

I wish that Thomas's cries of terror would drown out the disappointment that surges through me as I realize my dad hasn't been home for days. His usual parking spot out in the yard is still empty. My friends and I have been running around town so much that I didn't notice his absence. Nor have I seen him on the streets or in any shops.

He must have gone on a mail run early in the morning and

left without saying 'hello' or 'goodbye' like he normally would. My dad could have thought he'd be back before I woke. But the Mush got to him. There is no other explanation. He would have sent word if that wasn't the case.

It hurts to know that he won't be coming back ever again. I can only hope that his suffering didn't last long. However, since this fucking disease progresses so rapidly I doubt he was sick for long.

Now that I'm thinking about it, Copper had to get my dad sick.

The thought doesn't rest easy in my quivering stomach.

"Hurry the fuck up, Charlie!" Crista screeches as we abruptly stop mere feet away from the porch. My car squeals the moment I press hard on the brake. I jerk forward due to the force, close to slamming my head against the wheel.

Fresh blood from my split lip drips down my chin but I wipe it away quickly. I'll have to change the bandages later.

The sun has fully set by now, letting the darkness bloom into the sky and dampen whatever brightness that lingers. Such a shame. Normally I'd love to wallow in the dark with a horror movie playing on the TV. Unfortunately, the absence of sunlight encourages the fear I once relished in to grow and spread directly into my heart where I know it will attack.

"Fuck you!" I turn around in the seat to yell at her in return, rage coating my tone. My angered expression quickly disappears after taking in the sight of her gripping Thomas. I think my heart just cracked a bit more.

Her sweater is covered in all kinds of ugly fluid. The darker stuff that came up from his stomach and the lighter shit that keeps flowing from every part of his face. I swallow down a gag as she starts to cry again after he groans into her shaky

121

chest. Her thin pale fingers brush his frail sweaty hair away from his disturbing green eyes.

"Let's get him out." Bucky doesn't wait for a response before leaving the car.

I watch Crista adjust Thomas under her arms. She struggles to clutch his elbows. It's almost like he's too soft to grip. I see the way his muscles sink beneath her touch. All I can allow my body to do is slowly get out and into the rain. Why does it pour like this at the worst times?

I'm soaked again in an instant, a mere second.

Bucky assists Crista. They haul our friend with his arms loosely wrapped around their shoulders. I move ahead with my back facing the porch. My feet claw over the pebbled path and so do theirs.

Just as Thomas makes a gargling scream, I trip over the pebbles and land on the first three steps, cracking my back in a few places. The air in my lungs flees and struggles to return for a moment. My palms burn from the cuts I acquire as I attempt to catch my unexpected fall. I feel warm blood drip down my fingers as I stagger to my feet. The dark substance stains my jeans like fabric dye.

I'm going to say it will only get messier from here.

"Oh, Thomas!" Crista sobs as he slips from her and Bucky's hold, collapsing to his trembling knees.

He lands with a sickening thud. "L-Love bug?"

Those are the last words he will ever speak. But I am glad they are for Crista despite the newer wails of torment being shot into the downpour.

His elbows clash onto the path, the fragile skin tearing as his bones rip through it. It creates a sloshing sound that makes me cringe deeply. In a jerk, I hurriedly climb the porch steps while keeping my gaze on the scene before me.

Watching horror movies is already an odd habit I have. I may have wanted to one day film my own. But unwillingly being a part of the most grotesque thing ever is something else entirely.

Before I can properly stand on the steps Thomas starts to puke again. His body convulses like he's covered in a thousand ants, crawling all over him in little spurts.

"Shit!" Bucky curses as he jumps out of the way, taking Crista with him. Thomas suddenly stops moving, his skin now dripping off him.

"Oh, God!" Crista cries when what was once Thomas quickly peels apart, falling to the ground in a horrid slop.

An ugly gurgling noise erupts from the newly formed pile of mush. *Mush*. This time I can't contain the vomit that rises in my throat. I turn to the side, just barely making it off the steps before I empty my stomach again. The smell from that shit alone is enough for me to gag profusely.

Crista's shocking shriek jerks me upright. The disturbing green puddle starts to pulsate, and glowing mushrooms sliver to the surface, causing bits and pieces to flicker onto her and Bucky. I force a hand to cover my mouth. There is nothing left in me to puke.

A light seeps out of the spore-like holes in the clump of green goop, illuminating my friends who are covered in the remains of Thomas. Can it be called that? Whatever this Mush does, it changes people from the inside out until they aren't them anymore. I hate it with all my heart. Who created this shitshow? They must've been having a very, very bad day.

Silence soaks the air around us. The chirpy crows in the forest have now gone quiet. Winds tinged with warmth push

123

the rain at an angle, dousing everything in its path.

Bucky is the first of us to return to his senses. He carefully guides a shaking Crista around her dead boyfriend and over to me. She studies the now empty clothes that once were worn by a human being. Before I can get her in my grasp she rips away from Bucky to bend down low to retrieve Thomas's leather jacket.

"I'll wash it off." He offers his empty hands to her. I bit the inside of my cheek in anticipation. Will she freak out and have a total meltdown or will she realize that all he wants to do is help? I guess I'll find out.

I feel guilty when releasing a heavy sigh, consumed with relief as she gently nods her head.

"Go. I'll take care of her." I tell him, making sure to really look into his eyes.

He jerks his chin in answer but waits until I let Crista into the house before answering me.

"We just lost Thomas." His voice quivers.

I turn back to face him, tears now streaking down my heated face. I don't care to catch them.

"I know," I say. He doesn't speak anymore.

I help wash off the jacket. Pieces of the Mush slide off the worn black leather like slick oil, leaving suds behind. The smell of decay fills my nose, tickling my sinuses. I trap a sneeze in my nose by gripping my nostrils close for a few moments.

I do my best to avoid the squishy pieces of Thomas as the spraying water rushes over the expensive material. However, Bucky isn't so careful now that he's already covered in what used to be our close friend. I just hope none of it got in his mouth because it's all in his luscious curls and cheeks.

Damn, his jacket is pretty much ruined.

He loves that jacket.

Neither of us says a word when digging a hole to bury the strange pile of sick. I found a lone shovel near the back of the house. Bucky took it from my bleeding hands, his stern expression told me to back off and that he could handle it.

However, he gave me the honor of patting down the dirt. As I do this very thoughtfully I suddenly start hearing a distant moaning. At first, I think Bucky might have begun to cry. But when I look at him he also shares my confused expression.

I hold the shovel tight when spinning around. I give a sharp gasp after spotting a massive crowd limping across the front lawn and into the forest. The slowly moving horde trudges on covered in green muck. Their rotting stench clings to the inside of my lungs.

Their groans of pain are one thing, but their moans of purpose are another. They're on a mission. To whoever-the-fuck knows where and why.

Most of them limp in a staggered line while others barely flinch. I fear that their minds are no longer their own. This thing that has taken over their bodies has also infected their minds. It's such a damn shame too.

Anger fills my guts, burning my insides along with my spirit. I recognize over half of these people who quickly fall apart as the last make it through the tree line. Disgusting squishing sounds knock me out of the trance I was consumed by. That damn smell will never go away.

Bucky shakes his head with an irritated snarl. "This is fucked."

I nod in agreement.

"What are they doing? Where are they going? I hate not knowing anything." Bucky has a cute habit of asking the obvious questions. But are they the right ones? I guess we'll have to wait and see.

I toss the shovel next to my feet and adjust my favorite coat. A chilling breeze sweeps by, caressing my hair, and encouraging the curly gold strands to twist around my ears and neck.

"We follow," I tell him, giving him the camera that's been sitting on the front porch this entire time.

He doesn't bother to fight me on this; I'm glad for that.

I lead into the forest, following the trail of luminous green sludge that weaves between the lush cedar and pokey pine trees. My feet sink into the sour mud, the earth threatening to grip me tight and pull me under the ground. Maybe I should let it and be done with this fucked-up town.

Bucky talks to the camera. He's explaining what's just happened with our friend and this sickening group of ill people. Using poor Thomas as content for this documentary is wrong and cruel and yet it is necessary.

If this ever gets out, the people who surround the town and live in this country should know what the government does to its citizens. I just know deep in my heart that these CDC people did this. Exposing them seems like this is the right

126

thing to do.

We trail behind them. I keep close to the brooding sounds. My ears latch onto the quick pitter-patter of animals fleeing from the rotting horde. They got the right idea.

It doesn't take long until we reach the spot where my Copper melted into a puddle. There are no humans left. What lingers is a huge mound of Mush. A tremor-consumed pile the color of infectious snot has called a slight clearing in this forest its home. Its many large lumps quake and glow, a rhythmic strobe light in horror movie scenes where someone gets murdered with a butcher knife or something.

I originally thought the mushrooms on that white toad and the remains of Copper were big, but these fungi are at least twenty times their size. The thick stems sway in unison, slightly rotating counterclockwise. They glow as well, bringing this grotesque image together.

I make sure Bucky gets the most of the shot.

After taking a few pictures to hopefully brainstorm a movie poster we rush back.

I see Crista sitting on the steps of the porch. At first, I want to offer her a small smile filled with sadness. Maybe even go in for a huge that I most certainly dread giving.

But when I notice the slight green sheen of sweat above her brows and top lip my stomach twists into thick knots. I fail to walk any further towards her. My knees lock in place.

Bucky stalls behind me as I come to an abrupt stop. Tears sting at the rims of my eyes. This is too much for me to truly comprehend. Or maybe it's me who refuses to see what's right in front of me. This thing… the Mush is going to get us all, isn't it?

Me and Bucky are next.

Her voice is scratching as she croaks, "I'm c-cold."

14. And So The Villains Take The Lead

"Half the town is probably gone by now. And a shit tone of them basically evaporated into more gross shit. It's insane." Bucky does his best to explain to Crista.

She nods, grasping onto every word. Her quivering brows scrunch in concentration as she does her best to visualize what we saw back there.

I shake my head as she turns her gaze to me. "Look, the only way our questions will be answered is if we go to the source."

Her conflicted sigh tickles my insides. However, it's her choking cough that causes me to flinch on the steps of the porch. I made sure to hose it down before I took my seat. I don't want my old puke or the remains of Thomas touching me.

She wipes her nose onto her grubby sweater before marching toward the Impala. It looks like she made up her mind then. I give a heavy sign and follow after her. Bucky is not far behind me.

We trail in a unified line of sorts. The only problem is we're missing a vital member of Shocker Pictures. What a shame too.

"Walk next to the car." I hurry my words to stop Crista from even touching the door handle.

Her movement backward is jerky but otherwise coherent. "Got it."

I peer into the back seat. All the drying green puke and other disgusting fluids from Thomas still remain. If I'd forget the risk of getting sick a lot sooner than I want then she would be in the back.

However, there is no more luck for us in this world. She will be walking to April Square.

Crista keeps a determined face while trotting along the road. I keep the pace steady, listening to the engine rattle. All four windows have been rolled down to make sure she doesn't feel alone in this.

Plus, getting rid of this awful stench is better than nothing. And yet the sadness I feel for Thomas outweighs the irritation that I have for my ruined car. At least I now have my priorities set right.

Out of the corner of my eyes, I see her shiver, rubbing her arms from her chills despite how humid the outside is. Seeing her get sicker only fuels my frustration and anger. We better get answers or I just might throw some much-needed punches. And at this point, I don't care who I hit. I'm sure Buff Bucky will agree.

My hands flex around the stirring wheel. Even from here, I can hear her raspy breathing. It won't be long before her nose and ears start to leak.

More large army tanks stroll in the next lane the farther we get into town. The trees get fewer and the Mush piles start multiplying. I spot a few folks actually disintegrating from the sickness. Their cries of fear and agony will haunt my dreams and ultimately be nightmares.

The town really has gone to shit. It's all their fault.

I keep my eyes peeled for any faces that might stir panic in me. No one I truly know stumbles down the street or out of the various shops that are still somehow open. Due to the sound of my car a few store owners come up to the windows, searching for any signs of improvement for this disease. Their frowns of disappointment don't go unnoticed. Hell, I want to get the pieces to this fucking puzzle for all of us to put together.

Of course, those who haven't been infected yet are actively robbing any store they can. Many piles of glass litter the underneath of broken shop windows. Newspapers fly across the street from the whispering winds. Some store and bakery owners do their best to fight back against these thugs… these barbarians.

I think a lot of them went to high school with us. I guess

131

they didn't skip town to avoid this either. All they have left is to terrorize those who still linger here.

I'm not sure how useful that will be. None of us can leave town. What a bunch of idiots.

"Look, none of the CDC docs or nurses are even out this far from April Square." Bucky leans to whisper in my ear. "What the fuck are they even doing here if not helping?"

I give him a shrug as I continue to cruise onward. Crista started limping a few minutes ago. Despite her obvious turmoil, she stays close, occasionally glancing around, searching for something or someone. I don't blame her. Every second I imagine Thomas jumping out of an alley with a leaking bottle of spray paint and a mischievous smile on his face, clearly guilty of graffiti. That was his second favorite thing to do. The first was always going to be spending time with Crista.

She clears her throat and turns to look at me. Her tired eyes peek through her limp red bangs so terribly that I want to pout on her behalf. "What are you guys gonna do to get out of this?"

"Don't you mean what are 'we' going to do?" Bucky gives a shake of his head, indicating that she got her wording wrong. I don't think she did. I think we all know what's going to happen to her if we don't demand the CDC docs to fix her.

I scoff at his obvious denial.

She clicks her tongue at me. I roll my eyes and trudge on, ignoring the glare she shoots my way. Like I give a shit about whatever the hell she's going on about.

"We know that I'm not going to live through this. How are you going to get out of town?" Despite nearing the square Crista presses again.

This time I'm the one to make an annoying noise. I quickly step on the brake. The car jolts to a stop, almost sending Bucky into the dashboard. I don't bother to say sorry about it either as he struggles to brace himself.

I put the car in park before twisting in the seat. Holding my breath, I climb over Bucky to get really close to the window. His hands instantly cage in my hips. It takes great internal strength for me to ignore the way his fingers hook onto my pant loops. This guy is utterly insane for touching me like this and having no clue what it does to me.

Damnit, I need to focus.

"I get that you might be dying now, but that gives you no right to act like it. You are still walking and talking so there is a good ass chance the CDC has made a cure for the Mush. We just have to hang on long enough to get it for you. Now, any questions?" By the time I finish my little rant, I'm practically hyperventilating.

Crista gulps back a gag after another fit of hacks. She spits a gross loogy. I bit my lip to hide my own gag. No one needs my obnoxiousness.

"We square?" I ask. Too bad I can't offer my hand out to her. I rather not get the Mush from a simple handshake. That isn't rad at all.

"Alright, you're right." She rolls her shoulders. I have no doubt that they ache. I'm betting that all her joints are sore from just standing there.

Settling into my seat, I pat him on the shoulder. I just need the excuse to touch him more. He returns it by giving me a gentle squeeze on my thigh. It's an unusual touching moment for us. He's never done this before.

Instead of shrugging off his hold, I put the Impala in drive, letting his fingers carefully dig into my jeans that I'm pretty sure I've worn for the past three days. I'm not sure if we're in

September yet. Maybe it's still August. Who the fuck knows anymore.

The military personnel swarm April Square. They've even gated the entire place. I spot several checkpoints for those who are forced to enter.

Many crisp white tents litter the cobblestone area. Doctors in their pink hazmats are scattered about doing their weird scientist shit. Nurses are tending to the sick who occupy plenty of medical beds. I'm going to assume more are inside the tents. My eyes go wide once I realize that this is just what I can see from the front. There is no telling what beyond this.

My fingers tremble against the leather wheel. I think I'm freaking out. Not even Bucky touching me is going to make me feel any better.

I open my mouth to suggest we approach April Square from the east side. However, words stall in my throat when the car is suddenly surrounded by army folks. They come out of nowhere with rifles aimed right at us. My screams die in my mouth when the closest one shoves his hand into the open window and covers my mouth with a damp white rag. I'm forced to breathe in this tragic scent that I think I know of what.

This…this is a classic scene from hundreds of movies. I know what not to do in this type of situation. Unfortunately, instinct takes over and I inhale the chloroform. The chemical stings my nose and burns my esophagus, like hot knives digging into me.

I struggle against the hand gripping my head still.

This is utter bullshit. All I manage to do is give this fucker with a busted lip a death stare before I go unconscious.

15. Russians & Toads

My head is so heavy that I can't prevent it from leaning far onto my shoulder. I've got this crook in my neck that aches like a bitch. I try adjusting in this awfully uncomfortable wooden chair, attempting to open my eyes. However, my lids refuse to budge and whatever is wrapped around my arms prevents me from moving much at all.

Wait. What the fuck happened?

I hear a slight chuckle from across the room. Someone finds my struggles amusing. Asshole.

Actually, I'm going to guess that I've been put in one of those medical tents. The stench of pool float plastic clings to my sinuses. Hell, I'll take this smell over chloroform any day of the week.

The realization of it allows my eyes to shoot open. Harsh yellow light seeps into my vision, hurting me enough to groan. I think secretly wanting to be in a scary movie isn't really working out for me at the moment.

"Easy, Charlie. Don't want to give yourself a headache." The oddly comforting voice of Dr. Avery calls out to me. I hear the grin in her tone. Damn, it's this prissy bitch. Hasn't she had enough of our rain pours and gloomy clouds?

After a few moments of letting my achy body adjust to this new environment, I give her my very best death stare. It doesn't do much to sway her smug face. Hmm, what a pity.

Her tightly pinned-back black hair pulls her face taunt, exposing her prominent cheekbones. Gosh, she looks evil. Sounds about right.

She doesn't say anything else. Dr. Avery messes with her white coat before standing tall. Her looming features are toned down by the harsh lighting that honestly does nothing for her ivory complexion. After giving me a look of curiosity mixed with disgust she walks out of the tent, her strange heels clacking on the temporary flooring. The noise irritates me greatly.

Once I can no longer hear her footsteps, I shake violently in the chair. Whoever zip-tied me to this wooden chair took off my red jacket, letting the restraints dig into my wrists. I'm rubbing them raw, allowing for the thick white plastic to break my skin apart and cause blood to drip down my fingers.

I rock the chair to the side so hard that I bump into someone else into the one next to me. Blood splatter lands on me and this person's face.

"Bucky! Oh, shit. Wake the fuck up!" The sight of Bucky's gorgeous curly brown hair with those epic highlights wills me to shriek with pure glee. I've never been so happy in my life to see him.

He jolts awake. His big green-brown eyes soak in the overhead lights. His harsh breathing lets me know he's just as freaked as I am.

"W-Where the hell are we? Where's Crista? Oh, fuck my nose burns. Those dweebs need their asses handed to them." His worried voice makes my insides go numb.

I take a moment to gather my bearings. There isn't anyone here besides us. No sign of Crista.

Shit.

Instead, all I see is a lone table set up at the far side of the tent. A curious glint is what bothers me about this. I lean forward to get a better look. My hair slips over my shoulder as I do this, giving me a good look at the green gunk that managed to get on me.

About a dozen medical instruments dot the surface of it. The shine of their silver is unsettling. I don't want to know what these doctors are actually doing with the people of this town, my town for that matter.

The more shit I see from these people the more angry I get.

Before I can voice my ever-growing concerns the door flap of the tent opens and in comes the doctor again. I feel my lips dip into a menacing frown. I hope she burns in Hell for this because there is no way she is here to help us. I'd say she's in on this.

She takes the chair she sat in early and places it in front of us. I grip the arms of my chair tight as she offers me a wide smirk. The need to punch it off her face eats away at my insides. Despite my skin ripping at my wrists I tug against them far enough to growl in her face.

Yeah, that felt good.

Her throat clears. The sound of it makes me sick. Too bad I don't have the Mush to give to her.

"Look, I get that all of this appears bad. Well, it really is as bad as you think." She starts by addressing my first of many unanswered questions.

"So, you gonna tell us what the fuck is going on around here?" I don't bother to be nice about it either.

Dr. Avery tilts her head at my intense tone. Her strange cold eyes peer at me, doing their best to dig into my insides, my soul. What a fucking creep.

"Long story short is the way to go I suppose. I started an underground research and testing facility with a partner around twenty years ago. We chose Elora Falls as our home base because it's out of the way and hardly recognizable on a map. Plus, we would avoid the attention of the real CDC and government. We weren't exactly doing this legally. You see, Charlie, me and many of my colleagues were experimenting on reptiles and amphibians." She crosses her legs, getting comfortable as she says her fairytale story.

I jerk in the chair as she places a hand on my knee. If she thinks I'm going to willingly listen to this fucking bull then she's got another thing coming.

"Get off her!" Bucky literally spits on one of her heels. His saliva lands with a wet thump. She flinches in disgust.

I bite down hard on the inside of my cheek to hide my satisfied expression.

She squeezes my knee before continuing despite this recent display of defense.

"We had this grand idea to finally find a cure for cancer. We would be able to do this because we aren't afraid of testing the limits of science and man. And for a while, we were making such glorious progress. We were fucking months away from human trials for various versions of the cure. Hell, we even had vaccine-like medication to prevent the disease from festering in cancer-positive families. That was until young and curious Dr. Benson was approached by a Russian spy who somehow infiltrated our facility." Her bright green eyes suddenly darken. A cloud of disappointment and anger washes over them.

I can't bother to give her two shits about it.

My back aches from sitting in this strained position for who knows how long. There's a slight pain in my knees as well. Damnit, my stomach is grumbling lowly. Too bad there isn't any popcorn for this. Now that would have been a show.

Shit. Where did they put the camera? I hope they haven't figured out what we've been doing with it.

Then they'd really make sure we won't talk about any of this.

"She was somehow convinced to engineer a deadly strain created using various cancer samples. I'm guessing that most were from infected animals. Anyways, Dr. Benson made something so horrible that she planned to sell to the Russians for eighty thousand dollars. Poor woman thought she would have it all. Unfortunately, the first of her samples was compromised and made a toad specimen sick. I'm not sure how but it got out above ground before I could order it destroyed. We were lucky to get here before it managed to get out of Elora Falls." Dr. Avery genuinely looks distraught. I can't tell if it's real or not. I bet all the quarters in my black piggy bank that it's a no.

I wiggle my toes to keep them from cramping in my shoes. I'm so tired of this already. Just looking at her for so long makes my blood boil.

"We needed to pose as the CDC before the real corporation found out about this. Once we got a hold of a few infected citizens then our rapid testing began. It's terrible that all our tries for a cure and potential vaccine have failed. Now our mission is to completely eradicate this ugly sickness before it spreads to the rest of the state and eventually the country." That alone fuels my rage.

"You're going to kill off what's left of the town? Just like that?" Leave it to Bucky to voice my inner thoughts.

If I could I'd be crossing my arms in shame right about now.

Dr. Avery shakes her head. "It's not that simple."

"The fuck it ain't. Let me tell you something, doctor lady. We won't let you make us... This town, disappear due to your fucking mistakes!" I shout towards the end. My body shakes with anger and this sudden splurge of adrenaline.

"You're crazy." Bucky's nervous chuckle echoes into the tent.

The doctor who lied to us all, and let this happen under her watch, stands again. She fixes her crinkled lab coat. She says nothing as the door flap opens once more and in comes a very timid doctor with pale hair and hundreds of freckles on her face. That's when I realize this is the bitch who started all of this.

"You really wanted that moment, didn't you? You know after me and the town are gone you will be their next cleanup. Don't think you're in the clear just yet. I'd watch your back if I was you, Dr. Benson." She gulps nervously after I finish my speech.

It feels good to see her squirm.

I tilt my head to the side, allowing a wide grin to take over my face. "You aren't safe here either. You'll be dead probably by the end of the week just so they can get rid of the weak link. It happens in all the movies."

A ruckus laugh escapes me as a few of those fake military guys come inside the tent with their shiny black riffles.

"You fuckers are going to pay for this!" I screech at the top of my lungs, silently hoping the next town over can hear me.

Once again we're knocked out. Only this time by getting smacked in the head with the butt of their guns, hard. Everything goes blank and I somehow think I'm going to meet death on the other side of this dark abyss.

Act III

ACT
III

THE SAVIOR

16. Make It Out Alive

I 've been awake for about an hour now. A headache has taken root at the front of my skull. It pounds against my brain, fighting for me to go back to sleep. I clench my eyes over and over again to stay awake. My lungs hurt from inhaling that chemical the first time they made us go unconscious.

This time they moved us to a much different setting. I'm guessing it's an outside shed that connects to the underground facility. There's this large grate that rests in the middle of the concrete floor. I hear this occasional dripping coming from its depth. Either it's mold or moss that is scattered across it, resting stark against the metallic silver. It most likely has a ladder that leads to an entrance to that place.

Too bad for me that I'm chained up to this fucking cage that contains dozens of white toads with the Mush sprouting from their backs. I bet I look worse than them.

The glowing green light illuminates the room, coating the walls like brutally bright wallpaper. I've gotten used to the potent smell of rot. It lingers in my lungs, doing its best to infiltrate my mind and sink deep into my memories.

A clunky rustling noise catches my very tired attention. What is it now?

Bucky stirs at the other end of the room. Huh? I didn't even notice him near me this time. Damn, my entire body feels sluggish.

He jerks in his rusted handcuffs. He gravely curses at whoever put him in that awful position on the dirty floor. Nothing in me finds his struggles funny.

Once he sees me, his troubled expression morphs into a relieved grin. I know I should feel the same for him but I'm so tired.

"Charlie, are you alright?" His voice usually soothes me. It's gruff and satisfying.

I shrug and roll my throbbing eyes in the process. A few croaks from the toads add to this tragic atmosphere. I sort of feel awful for the ugly little creatures. They didn't ask for this to happen to them either. Something we have in common.

144

"This is the end of us." It's not a question.

His scoff is a nice touch to listen to.

"Bullshit. What the fuck is wrong with you?" Bucky's sudden anger causes my skin to gain goosebumps. I fight against a shiver that does everything to shoot down my spinal cord.

"Look where we are. There is nothing we can do to get out of here or save whoever is left." I lean forward with a slight growl.

I've never been one to give up. But after seeing the Mush destroy Elora Falls and its people I can't see a way out of this mess. Why doesn't he see that too? It'd be better if he realized that now rather than later.

He gives a chuckle filled with disbelief. "Now that isn't the Charlie that I know and love."

Hmm. *Love*. Not something I ever thought he would say to me.

The word love is strange coming from him. I've never heard him say it before. My heart aches knowing it isn't the type of love that I feel for him. Jeez, watching him play on the football field for the first time was magic. The way he worked with the team and guided others into a more positive path sparked something in me. Then as he started to hang out with us after becoming Shocker Pictures he'd gaze at me intensely when the others weren't looking.

I never thought it was supposed to mean more than just a glance.

Sometimes he'd let his hand touch mine when passing each other in the halls. I'd have to hide my smirk as he went to his jock buddies while I found the theater kids. No one besides Shocker Pictures knew we even hung out with Bucky. And yet he made sure to always let me know he was secretly with us.

145

Now that's good acting.

Hell, when some blonde bimbo tripped Crista during a pep rally he stopped what he was doing to help her. That raised some questions with his team who enjoyed messing with us freaks.

And yet this 'love' he's talking about is nothing more than the friendship kind.

Despite my scoff tears stream down my heated face. I didn't even feel my eyes sting with them this time. That goes to show how out of touch I'm being.

"Get out of that head of yours just for two seconds and listen. We can get out of this because you are a badass. Where's the chick that breaks the noses of the homophobes and isn't afraid to tell people to stick it where the sun don't shine? I know you're tired and defeated, but don't give up. Not yet. Please, for me." His words attempt to seep into my mind.

They fail to convince me of anything.

I shake my head quickly. There's nothing he can tell me that will convince me that we can make it alive. I don't see how that's possible.

Sighing, I cross my legs. My rusted handcuffs clink around the steel bar of the toad cage. Their sounds of discomfort are somewhat pleasant. Good to know I'm not the only one suffering. Well, now that just sounds so pathetic.

Bucky curses under his breath and tries breaking the cuffs. He gives them a few tugs but they don't budge.

"I love you, Charlie Everett. I may have made some questionable romance choices in school, but you have always had my eye. I was just afraid of people thinking I was using you for something like getting good grades or letting you write my essays for me. And believe me, they would throw those accusations my way during practice all the fucking time." Bucky starts to smile. It makes me cry harder.

My sobs fill the room. It doesn't discourage him from continuing.

"I admire the way you carry yourself so freely. You support people no matter what and stand up to those who have small minds. Gosh, what's not to love about you? Don't even get me started on that damn red raincoat of yours. It goes perfectly with your curly blonde hair and forest-green eyes. Damnit, Charlie. I need you to hear me. We can do this. I know it." Something inside me cracks.

Then it shatters completely.

Whatever dam has been blocking the flow of my badassness has somehow broken into a thousand pieces. And that lets my mind wander to those we have already lost.

The pain I felt for Thomas surfaces back and shifts into a rage. I grunt as I yank my cuffs madly. The rusted chains squeal a sickening shout. The noise echoes into the room.

I don't want to give up. I'm tired of the Mush and these fake CDC assholes getting ahead of us. Elora Falls might be filled with people who can't seem to find sympathy for others and outsiders, but it doesn't mean they deserve to die because of a stupid doctor's mistake.

This isn't fair. Bucky is right. We have to do something.

Getting on my knees I grip the chain to the cuffs and pull back with all my might. The cage of toads groans as I use all the force I can muster.

"Fuck yeah. That's my Charlie!" I hear Bucky exclaim and his cuffs rattle as well.

This sparks a smile to grow on my face. I use this fuel to break the chains. A harsh snap fills the air and I land on my backside. I huff when getting back to my feet. Jeez, my bones ache something fierce.

My arms throb from that annoying sitting position but otherwise, I feel fine.

Bucky still struggles with his. I gently sprint over to him and grip them too. Together, we jerk the chain and they crumble. Looks like these doctors aren't very smart. They probably should have tied us up with those zip ties. Now that would have worked wonders.

Despite the torn flesh on my wrist and blood-stained skin, I feel somewhat empowered by all that he said.

"What now?" Bucky asks. He shakes his ruined letterman jacket, letting dusk fly off.

"Well, we find Crista. She could still be alive. I don't want her to die of the Mush without her at least knowing that we're okay." I tell him.

He nods in agreement. I do the same in return.

Now all that's left to do is get out of this shack. I glance around for a moment. My lips shift into a grin once I spot a crowbar resting against the back wall. As I said, these docs are such idiots. Who leaves a possible weapon near prisoners? Amateur villains.

17. Biting The Green Dust

T his place is crawling with these sick fucks. I wish I had
been taken by little green aliens. Anything is better
than being even within ten feet of them.

Despite April Square being taken over by dozens of tents and
many military vehicles I still have a sense of where everything
is. So, I am the one leading Bucky in circles trying to find
where they might be keeping Crista. His fingers tightly clutch

the back of my coat that I found hanging on a hook outside the shed door, letting me guide him forward. I'm glad that he trusts me enough to follow with a blind eye.

We've accidentally run into a few tents that house people who don't have the Mush. Not yet at least. I'm sure they will all have that grotesque fate. I won't be surprised if we catch it too. Even though they aren't sick the doctors are still performing all kinds of tests on them. Most are hooked up to various machines. The annoying beeping clicks into the air, agitating some of the patients.

I don't blame them for shooting glares at these people. I do the same every chance I get.

They may be looking for a cure for this. Or they're searching for a way to quickly kill us off using the Mush and hopefully make us disappear. Neither of those possibilities sounds good.

After running around with bent knees we managed to find a secluded spot behind the nearest supply tent. I yank Bucky behind me to keep his large frame out of sight.

A while ago a slight alarm had gone off. Many security guys in black uniforms rush around, most likely looking for their escaped prisoners. Us.

"What are we going to do now? We haven't found Crista." Bucky's warm breath wraps around my neck. Goosebumps flare on my flesh. I roll my shoulders to get rid of this funky itch.

"Give me a minute, I'm thinking." That sounded more gruff than I intended for it.

He scoffs but doesn't try arguing. Good for me.

A bright yellow searchlight flies over the tops of the tents, causing the white plastic roof and sides to shine. I shield my eyes from the intense glare. But before my vision is blocked completely a quick flash of pink catches my attention.

Bucky notices my change in posture. I can feel his confused gaze pointed at my suddenly straight spine. Sitting in a crouched position for so long makes me feel like a hunchback.

"Look, over there." I carefully point to another supply tent across from us. It's a stark contrast to the dark cobblestone. The front flap had been pinned to the top, letting me see straight inside and at the pink hazmat suits.

He catches my line of sight and groans lowly.

"You can't be serious?" He sounds worried.

"If we wear the suits then we can move around April Square freely, duh." I roll my eyes at the obvious answer to his question. If I think about it, no one will stop us if we just casually check the tents to ensure everything is alright.

It's actually the perfect cover. It's a good thing that various movie scenes with this same concept flash into my mind. They offer the best guidance at the worst times. I guess television doesn't always cause brain rot.

"Shit." He doesn't complain.

I wait till the coast is clear before sprinting across the path and into the tent. Bucky is right behind me, unraveling the tent flap to shut us inside.

I retrieve a suit from one of the hooks. It feels slick in my hands, almost like how I'd imagine a snake to be. It has this odd sparkle to it as well. It shines like a small rainbow that hangs in the clouds over the forest after a harsh rain. Those are the best.

"Turn your back," I order him. He grunts in response.

It takes some maneuvering but I manage to get the suit over me and my clothes. I have to tuck my coat around my body snug enough to zip the suit.

We help each other out with securing the large spacious helmet. Next, we find the little air tanks that connect to the yellow tubes that flow direction into these pink contraptions. Bucky flips the on switch for my tank and I inhale the insanely sterile air. I take too much in, making me cough.

Bucky roughly pats my back to get me to shut up.

"S-Sorry," I mumble.

"S'okay. Let's get the fuck out of here and find our friend." Bucky lets a soft smile take over his lips.

It should be enough to get some motivation coursing through my veins. And yet all it does is allow a frown to consume me. I won't allow myself to feel a moment of relief until this is all over. And even then I won't feel alright. I'm sure this will scar us both for the rest of our lives.

Wearing these suits really does come in handy. We're able to move freely around here. No one stops to question our assignment. I think it's an utter miracle.

Eventually, I end up spotting a large medical tent. This time it's fully pink instead of the typical white of the ones around it. It has multiple rooms and a high ceiling. How did we not catch this earlier?

Right at the entrance is a large sign with reflective writing that has been posted. It says:

Beware.
Infectious patients inside.
Enter at your own risk!

Too bad I tend to avoid warning signs. Especially during football season where I'd take Shocker Picture onto the field to trash the stands and get it on film. Those were some fun nights until the sheriff and his deputy showed up and put us in jail for the night.

We take one more look around before carefully walking inside. Despite the thick suits on our bodies, I can feel the drop in temperature. I'm guessing it's cold in here to keep their fevers down. I wonder if it's been doing any good.

I thought the people being kept in the experiment tents were bad, but this is so much worse. The green stuff leaking from the rows of infected people glows, creating a united light to spread across the inside of the tent. However, there is a challenge to this with the bright blue that's coming from the stuff they're pumping into them.

They all have a thick tube inserted into their neck. The sight of it makes me squirm.

Most are in the late stages of the Mush. Some are close to being a puddle. Bucky is beside me as we gently walk down the aisle of at least twenty medical beds.

I pick up pace as I spy unruly red hair at the far end on

153

the right side. Crista had been placed at the back of the tent, having us go deeper into this bullshit.

My eyes go wide at the troubling sight of my close friend. She's limp under those crisp white hospital sheets. They dressed her in a pale purple medical gown. There are stitches on her arms and neck. They must have examined her internally, wanting to know what the Mush is doing to her insides as she still lives.

Such sick fucks.

The thought makes me barf a little in my mouth. Stomach acid coats my taste buds. I swallow it down hard to focus on the task in front of me.

Her eyes are half closed. Her hair is sweaty against her pale forehead. All her many freckles are so faint. Crista is a ghost.

I fight against the tears that swell in my eyes as I carefully grasp her frail hand in my gloved one. Her bones are prominent beneath her green-tinted skin. She doesn't have long at all.

"Crista? It's me, Charlie." I speak to her softly.

At first, she doesn't budge. I give her hand a gentle shake. "Crista?"

Then she manages to wiggle in her sleep. Her eyes open wider to reveal that familiar green haze over them. I hate this for her. It must feel awful to be consumed by the Mush. I never wanted this for her or the people of Elora Falls.

She opens her cracked lips to say something. I can barely hear as she says, "Marshmallow."

I glance over at Bucky. He has no idea why she said it. He shrugs his shoulders at me. Well, at least she said something.

"Crista, it's me and your other friend Bucky. We came to rescue you." He inhales sharply behind me.

We both know Crista won't be getting out of this tent alive. That realization finally lets my stubborn tears slip down my face and drip off my chin, hitting the bottom of the mask. I didn't want her to see me like this, a broken mess. It seems that she isn't even in her right state of mind to care anymore. Perhaps that's the best thing for her.

"You look like Slimer. Well, if that ugly little green bastard had a pink cousin." Her voice is filled with a childish giggle.

At least I can say that she finally watched *Ghostbusters* like I asked her to three years ago. But I think bringing it up now might not be the best time for it. I'll take it anyway.

Her laughter turns into harsh hacking, resulting in her jolting forward to projectile vomit dark green goo all over my front. I feel the puke pattering against me and slip off onto the cobblestone ground. I gulp down my own vomit. No need to get the inside of this suit messy.

I'm so glad I can't smell anything outside this hazmat.

"P-Pretty kitty," Crista mumbles to herself when sitting back on the bed. Whatever they've been giving her has scrambled her brain. She has no idea who I am or Bucky.

I give a curt sniffle. "It's been good to see you. I don't think you'll be alive in a few hours so I'll just say this now. I love you very much. I may have been angry that you and everyone else planned to leave this place, to leave me. But you would have been the best fucking screenwriter in history. I always felt that in my gut. If I make it out of Elora Falls I will make sure people know you and Thomas. You can make that a promise."

The tears keep coming, staining my cheeks. They feel like knives digging into my flesh and heart.

"Don't worry about us. Go to sleep, Crista. Everything will be alright." I hear the sad smile in his voice. Bucky's words seem to soothe her, guiding her into a sleep just like he said.

Good. She won't see us potentially get murdered by these doctor freaks or die of the Mush.

"Where the fuck did our suits go?" A strangled shout echoes outside the tent. My body jolts from the disrupting sound.

Shit. I didn't even think that these would belong to someone.

Neither of us says anything more. Bucky searchers for the back door flap. Once he finds it he quickly unzips it. I give her my best smile. It's full of hope, warmth, and love for her. Wherever she goes after dying I want it to be filled with chunky sweaters and many pretty flowers that bring out the color of her eyes. Yeah, I think she'd like that very much. Maybe she will somehow be reunited with Thomas. Now I would kill to see that.

We both strip out of the suits and leave them in the tent as we flee. Jeez, why do I suddenly feel like a criminal? This situation will never improve.

18. For The Love Of Football Players

V arious trash fires are scattered around the eerie empty
streets of Elora Falls. The corrupt flames illuminate
the windows of shops and seep inside to make the
walls glow.

I've got a good feeling that the teens who were left to do
whatever they wanted started this mess. They broke into the
street stores, cleared out the cash registers, and created the

ultimate chaos. Jeez, wasn't the Mush enough for them?

The dark blue sky is littered with stars. Occasionally, I like to look above me and count them. It eases my mind to know there are people in this world who aren't faced with this horror like Bucky and I. No matter what, this shit better not get out and scare everyone else.

There haven't been any surprise jumps from the fake CDC either. All of them are centered around April Square. I haven't heard an alarm about us being missing either. At this point, they might think we're dead.

That might be the best thing for us.

"Can we stop walking? I'm exhausted." Bucky groans next to me.

I roll my eyes. It's a movement filled with irritation. I'm tired too. But not enough to mope around and complain about it. There isn't time for that.

"Fine. The Blockbuster is up ahead. We can squat there for a while until we can get out of this place." My voice is scratchy as if flows up my throat.

"Thank fuck." Bucky's use of curse words is getting more frequent. I guess he can say whatever he wants since his father isn't around to smack him across the face for it. He never hit Bucky hard enough to cause any bruising or broken bones. Well, his father rarely lost his cool. He did everything to appear calm and collected. But when it came to football fumbles and fights on the field, he was a monster.

I gasp as we come face to face with one of our favorite places. All the windows have been shattered. Many of the shelves holding thick VHS tapes are on the tiled floor. A few of the overhead lights flicker in and out. This is a truly spooky scene. I never thought any of this would be possible. It's like I woke up in an apocalyptic world.

Bucky tries to get the door to open. The hinges moan in protest. After another attempt, Bucky gives up with a huff. "Won't open."

I nod in understanding before carefully climbing into the shop through the jagged window. A few stray glass pieces slice through my palms and jacket sleeves, tearing the already ruined material. Blood seeps down my fingers, dripping onto the floor as I walk further inside. I ignore the sting and yet welcome the new sensation. It seems to flush out the cloud that has been hovering over my mind, knocking some real thoughts in me.

"I'm going to clean up. I starting to hate the feeling of Mush all over me." I don't give him a chance to say anything. My feet crush glass as I limp down the main aisle to the bathroom in the back.

I lock the door behind me once I'm inside. The harsh yellow light cascades over me in a quick blink. I'm forced to squint until my eyes adjust to the brightness. In doing so I accidentally peer into the long mirror that has been fixed above the cracked porcelain sink.

A real bad move on my part.

A grimace sets upon my battered face. My eyes are still black and purple. Jeez, even my lips are busted even more. I guess I really did take a beating. The sudden thought of Jake rushes into my mind. The image of him hanging on the tall sharp fence causes my stomach to roll. He might've been a massive dick, but that didn't mean I wanted to see him die like that.

I give a big huff and twist the knobs of the faucet. Warm water spews out of the spout, hitting my freshly cut hands. The sharp sting shocks me. I hiss in pain. However, I rather be cut a thousand times than die of the Mush. Maybe Jake going out like he did was a small mercy. Now he won't get the chance to be sick.

After the water no longer runs pink I move on to scrub my arms and aching face. I feel various chunks of the Mush and dirt slide off of me and into the sink. That's when the sense of overwhelming disbelief turns into a sudden realization for me.

I bite the inside of my cheek to keep from sobbing. Hot tears leak from my cloudy eyes. Not even putting on my ruined coat makes me feel any better. I've lost two best friends of mine. Thomas went out so horribly.

Oh, my Crista. It's unfair that she didn't get to live her life either. None of this situation has been fair and I need to stop wishing for it to be.

That will get me nowhere. Just a few more miles and me and Bucky will be out of this fucking town.

"You good in there?" Bucky's deep sultry voice breaks through the door. It startles me enough to crash my back into it. I give my body the go-ahead to slowly drag down. I cross my knees once the cool tile hits me through my rugged jeans.

I give a sickening sniff. "Yeah, all good."

That is such a lie. I'm falling apart and I don't know how to pick up the pieces. This shouldn't be happening at all. Don't people know that the mistakes they make almost always affect others? Those doctors, especially Dr. Avery, should have seen this coming. If they were as smart as she makes them out to be then this would have been prevented.

I guess they're a shit show too.

"I know that we've seen some insane shit, but we're almost

out of this dump. Just a little bit more walking and then we'll be fine. Charlie?" His words fail to soothe me.

"Oh, yeah? I'd be surprised if we aren't eaten alive by infected toads or something like that." I have no idea where all this negativity is coming from. Actually, I do and it's called the fucking Mush.

His irritated snicker vibrates the door. I guess he's sitting on the other side of it. If it wasn't there our backs would be touching. The very idea of us touching makes my skin crawl and my chest get all warm. I hate this reoccurring feeling.

"Keep thinking like that and we definitely won't make it out of here alive," He tells me. I hear the grin in his voice.

"Okay, say we do get out of here, what are we supposed to do after? I sure as hell ain't going to be begging for scraps on street corners or offering my virgin pussy on a silver platter. Any bright ideas?" I could have kept that last part to myself. However, remembering the cousin my dad said had used to be a street worker gives me the option I really want to avoid.

"Damn. You're fucking psycho, Charlie Everett." Bucky says in a lighter tone.

"Yeah, but you love it," I say back.

There is a slight pause to fill the air. A silence that offers out its hand for me to take. But he is the one to snap that hand in two before I can lock my fingers with it.

"I love you." He sounds so sure.

I don't force my grin back as I respond, "I love you too."

His chuckle is music to my ringing ears. Such a pleasant sounds. I'd rather hear this a thousand times over than the tortured moans coming from the quarantine camp in April Square.

"I mean it," I say.

161

"Yeah, I've known about that for a while too." He says back.

A little fluttering feeling erupts in my stomach. I think this is what the movies mean when they describe butterflies. I'm not sure if I should hate it or adore it. Damn, I need to get a grip. Of course, they aren't real, it's just my body reacting to what the hell is going on between us.

His deep sigh rattles my bones. My spine tingles with anticipation. How am I so affected by this when I can't even see him? Hmm. Love is utterly strange and different with him.

"Alright, get outta there so I can finally kiss you." His demand is quickly met.

I rush to my feet, slipping on the tiles, and scramble to unlock the door. I'm not given the chance to say anything else as Bucky grips the sides of my heated face and pulls me close. A slight whimper tries to push out of me as our lips collide. It's a lot wetter than I imagined, but so warm and oddly comforting. This is what I've been missing out on.

Something hard hidden in his jeans presses against me. I'm not an idiot. I know exactly what it is and that knowledge encourages a flush to erupt all over my battered skin.

If only majestic fireworks or a cannon could go off in the background then this might be the perfect scene.

My lungs clench and I'm forced to tear myself away from him. A wicked grin spreads across his now-swollen lips. It's a wonderful sight.

A shocking noise quickly shatters the moment. Three gunshots ring out, coming from April Square. Now that tingle in my spine has sunken into pure dread.

19. Badass Movie Montage

"Y ou good?" Bucky attempts to rub my arms up and down as a motion of comfort.

I back away from him, taking a few steps forward under the still-blinking lights. My heart races and not from our shared kiss we had moments ago.

It's not rocket science to know what they were shooting at. Either killing off patients who are too far gone to continue testing or the few who are not sick yet tried to escape their prison camp. I don't want to take a chance and only assume one of these is right.

Something in me pushes against my heart. At first, I think it's hunger. I'm not sure when was the last time I ate. I give Bucky a small smile before moving around him to search for the checkout counter. I'm relieved to find most of the candy and Cheez balls are still here. I take a blue can and start munching on them. Bucky does the same. His crunching on the delicious cheese snacks fills the void that is this bizarre silence.

"The gears in your head are spinning wild. Wanna let me in on what you're thinking this time?" Bucky mutters through a mouth full of Cheez balls.

Is it that obvious I'm thinking so hard? Well, I'm considering something that will surely get us both killed if we're caught. But I know it will be worth all the tears and sweat we've shed so far. All I need to do now is convince him. It shouldn't be a problem, I hope.

I wipe my fingertips clean onto my jeans, smearing the bright orange substance from the cheese snacks over the soiled fabric.

"We need to go back and release the people who aren't sick. It's not fair to keep the sick there either but maybe the rest have a chance. It would give us more opportunity to spread the word about what went wrong with this place since we don't have the camera anymore. Okay, maybe the documentary was doomed from the start, I get it. I just want to do something good in the middle of all this evil." I can't believe I let myself ramble like this. I hate rambling. It's the lack of self-control of the mouth. That's something I never let go of.

He squints down at me. Bucky drops his empty can on the floor, kicking it far away from him. It clashes with something and a sharp pitch echoes into the ruined store. I do my best to keep myself from flinching.

He mumbles a quick apology. I smile at him.

Bucky clears his throat. "Umm, well. I don't think it's the best idea you've come up with, Char."

I chuckle at his reluctance to see my new vision for us and the rest of the town. Then I notice him fiddle with something in his pocket. "What's that?"

The ex-football player perks up, the corner of his lips hitching high in a smirk. I can't figure out if I should be intrigued or worried.

He fishes out the mystery object. My brows furrow as he slips out a black tape. Bucky flips it in his hands for a moment before I realize what it is.

"Holy shit!" I jerk it from him, the surprisingly warm plastic burning through my palm. "How did you get this."

"I think Thomas shoved it in my pants before collapsing in front of the porch. He was one sneaky bastard." Bucky's eyes darken for a split moment.

I nod in understanding. Leave it to the troublemaker of Shocker Pictures to somehow manage to practically save those who are left. He's probably flipping us off or throwing a spray paint bottle from the afterlife if there is one.

"We doing this?" I wrap my hair in a high ponytail with a random hair tie I found in my coat pocket. My bangs are crusted with blood and green goop so they won't be moving much.

It can give hairspray a run for its money.

"I guess we are." Bucky shakes his head and moves around me to head to the front door.

With a massive grin on my face and the song 'Eye of the

Tiger' by Survivor playing in my mind, we both creep out of the busted Blockbuster and carefully walk to the hunting and hiking supply store a block away. The warm summer air grazes my face on the way there. My feet ache but I ignore the pain in an instant when the rusted hanging sign of the shop comes into view. I've got a feeling that there is gonna be some crazy shit in this place.

I wonder what Dr. Avery would like to be assassinated with. Because I do plan to take her down. Basic human morals be damned.

Surprisingly, the store is completely untouched. Racks of bows and arrows are still full along with the glass cases of guns and ammo. The walls are made of dark wood which creates a very cozy atmosphere in here despite all the hunting weapons. Pale white lights hang from the ceiling. The black tile flooring is a grand contrast to the massive white back wall that has many taxidermy animals on display.

Bucky moves to the arrows, his eyes sparkling from the urge

to inspect them and find a bow he wants to use. I know that curious look from anywhere. He wears the same expression when studying the opponents on the field.

I want to use something more dramatic. My feet carry me to the front. I see a few handguns in the cases. Moving around them, I find the smallest one and break the glass with my elbow. The sharp pieces shatter into the case. I'm lucky the owner never opted for alarms. Mr. Tanner really did not like to use technology.

The weapon feels cold in my hands. I warm it with my body heat for a moment before taking a box of ammo and filling the clip. After that, I shove it in the back of my pants. I move over to the next case, break it, and fetch the sharpest knife I see. It feels light and will be easy to use.

"Wait, we can't just go back in that shit lookin' like this." Bucky whisper-shouts from across the store.

I lean over the cases to get a better view of him. "What do you suggest?"

He shrugs his shoulders a bit. I follow his adjusted line of sight to the various clothing racks that litter the main space. Most are camo shirts, pants, and jackets. Others are plain-back shirts.

Ahh, I get what he means. With a curt nod from me, Bucky moves forward and starts to pick out his camo attire. He shuffles around the racks and stacks of random hiking supplies such as rope and tents to find the changing room.

Placing my weapons down for the moment, I too find a pair of cargo pants with an interesting forest print. I don't bother to go to the dressing rooms. I strip out of my ripped jeans and replace them with these pants. Next, I take off my graphic tee and red coat and toss them onto the floor. I choose a medium black shirt, slide it over my head, and tuck it. Now all I need is some black face paint to signal war and I'll be square.

I wad up my coat and hold it firmly.

A throat clears behind me. There he stands in the same outfit with a can of literal black and green face paint. He's already got some smeared onto his cheeks and nose.

"I figured this would fit that little movie playing out in your head." His smile is large enough to show off his pearly white teeth.

With a soft sigh, I place my favorite coat onto the nearest case without any intention of ever picking it back up again. It's the end of a truly dramatic era of mine. I think it's best if I don't wear it. By now I'm sure Dr. Avery will be expecting a girl wearing red to run around town. It's smart to leave it behind.

He notices me do this without hesitation. Bucky gives me a slight nod of approval.

I grin right back at him and take the small can from his hands. Digging my finger into the smooth paint, I run it across my face. It feels slightly heavy. That will come in handy to keep me grounded.

I place the gun back inside my pants and stuff the knife into the pocket nearest to my right hand.

There will be a fight. I feel it deep in my bones. This Dr. Avery won't go without one. And maybe that's alright with me. Perhaps I've been begging for one since the start of this shit show.

Before we leave the store I grab a machete just in case and shove it into a pocket of my pants too.

Our footsteps click on the cobblestone street. All the trash fires still burn, their bright flames licking close to the dark sky.

I inhale the moist wind that blows against us. It ruffles my hair, causing the long curly strands to stick to my damp neck.

The heat is rising and so is my determination. The summer weather is a nice touch.

We will get these people out. I will happily die trying. Bucky is on the same page. He carries a rifle close to his chest. His perfect face is like a stone as he marches at my side. Damn, Crista would have loved this. She had a secret flare for the dramatic. I guess that's why we got along so well.

And of course, Thomas would be the one to announce our presence with his loud iconic laughter. Shit, I miss him too.

20. Back From The Dead

I move like a mysterious black cat under a full moon. Stealth has always been an advantage of mine. I can be silent when I must, especially when trying to avoid my dad when coming home so late that the sun starts to rise above the trees. This time is no different.

The shiny silver machete is kept close to my chest as we scamper around with bent knees. It's not hard to stay behind these massive ugly tank military tanks and white medical tents. Groups of false soldiers move in staggering rhythms, making it nearly impossible to get past them.

Bucky peers around the vehicle. His being way taller than me is useful.

"The tent is empty. They're not there anymore." Releasing the prisoners first to ensure chaos was the first part of the plan. Damn, that's unfortunately a smart move on their part. I hate that.

"What the hell does that mean?" I lean around his bronze shoulder to get a look for myself. Before we even got close to the Square he ripped off the sleeves of his shirt. I don't mind his display of skin. It's pleasant to watch the street lamps shine down on his soft yet muscular flesh.

And I'm positive he wanted me to look at him because Bucky made sure I could see his semi-permanent smirk. He's so full of himself that I force myself to suppress a giggle.

None of the guards are there around the front tent flaps. It's wide open to display empty cots and bare tables.

"Where did they take them?" I mutter while looking elsewhere.

Pounding footsteps make their way over to us. I tug on his belt loop and drag him behind me in a quick sprint. We stall behind the newly empty tent, panting on our knees, feeling frustration.

Sweat drips down my face, mixing in with the paint. I'm glad I didn't decorate my eyelids with it or else I'd have vision loss with it seeping into my eyeballs.

My gaze searches around the base camp soaking up anything newly suspicious. Most of the medical personnel are packing up, gathering all remaining supplies, and shoving them into the big trucks. Looking around I notice a few of them, men, discussing something really heated.

One of them mimics I guess throwing a football. He looks like a moron. How did even move his arm in that awkward angle? I've never seen Bucky throw a football like that.

A small gasp escaped my lungs. I grip Bucky's arm in realization.

"They took them to the football field. I don't have a fucking clue why but these idiots just told us in such little words, right in front of us." My smirk only widens as I watch the same guys pretend to tackle each other in their bubblegum pink hazmat suits.

Crista was right. These freaks do look like Slimer's cousin.

"Probably too many people with the Mush to keep in the tents. The field has enough space to house the entire town. It makes sense." He shrugs his shoulders, his brows furrow in consideration.

Yeah, they're at the football field alright.

"C'mon," I speak to make sure the way is clear before scuttling from out behind the tent.

Bucky is hot on my tail. I feel his warm breath kiss the back of my neck. I bite the inside of my cheek to hide my grin as his hands graze anything part of me they can.

My feet in these muddy Converse ache but it doesn't stop my hurried pace toward the high school.

The bright streetlamps that line the field shine down onto the green grass and make the strands almost glow.

We creep around the chain fence that surrounds the stands. Our shadows are cast across the ground, sticking close like some kind of parasite. It could be worse I'm sure.

It's not hard to spot the twenty-something people in the middle of the field with their hands cuffed in zip ties. Their bound hands are connected with more of the ties, keeping them stuck together with no chance of escape.

Fuck, that must be a terrible experience.

My stomach knots as we get closer to the back gate. My eyes water at the sight of at least a dozen red gasoline cans scattered around them. Now I notice that the towns folk are covered in that shit, soaked to the bone with it. Anger floods all my senses completely.

With a huff, I sneak into the large hole in the fence that's closer than the gate.

Bucky curses as he catches me tripping on the jagged pieces of fence that snag my pants. It doesn't slow me down even for a second.

"Don't you dare!" His whisper-shout doesn't penetrate my

mind at all.

I see red, it coats my vision. Nothing in me can stop me from standing up straight and strutting forward. Once I spot who I'm looking for I know there is no going back.

Dr. Avery is standing on a small wooden podium speaking to them. All I can really hear through the pounding in my ears is, "This must be done for the good of science."

Before I get close enough to sneak up behind the bitch an elderly woman by the name of Willie Marmalade snickers in disgust. Which happens to be a good surprise. She owns the cupcake shop a few blocks down from the elementary and hates conflict with a passion.

"It was science that failed. None of this would've happened if you all kept to the universal moral code of not fucking everything up." The purple bruise on her wrinkled cheek seems to turn darker as she lifts her head. Those silver short curls of hers blow in the wind.

Damn. I'm glad someone said it other than me.

I open my mouth to agree only to stop abruptly at two oddly familiar people who move closer next to Dr. Avery. I didn't notice them earlier. I haven't seen them at all since the start of this. They've been hiding. What little fuckers.

The first is a tall black man with short salt-and-pepper hair. His pale mustache wrinkles. Is that Bucky's dad? No, I don't believe it. But after squinting my eyes I can make out the same scrunched brows he and his son share. Yeah, it's him.

The other has long curly red hair close to the shade of blood. I get a sneak peek of her chilling green eyes. My chest squeezes at the sense of deep familiarity.

Instead of attacking them, I step aside and allow Bucky to catch up with me. He takes my right hand and gives it a tight squeeze.

A few of those tied notice our new presence. They don't give us expressions of relief. They only grow sadder. This causes the attention of the others to turn towards us. I gulp deeply, wishing I'd choke on my own spit. Anything to get this over with.

"Dad?" I was right. His dad squares his shoulders and dips his head. Oh, like that's going to make things better.

"Sorry, son." He tries to reason. All Bucky does is scoff in embarrassment. I don't blame him for it. I'd be so pissed if my dad did that to me. Maybe it's a good thing he's dead.

As if things couldn't get any worse, I make brutal eye contact with the other mysterious person. I feel the color actually drain from my face. A dangerous chill washes over my spine and I'm suddenly breathless.

This can't be happening. No way is this real. No, the Mush killed me and I'm really in Hell receiving torture.

Don't believe it, Charlie. She's not really there standing in front of you looking like a gaping fish out of water. Even after telling myself this, I know this is fucked.

My heart races as I quickly catch a glimpse of those dark freckles. I know this woman and she should be dead, buried in the ground in Elora Falls cemetery.

Wow. I might faint.

"Mom?"

21. Failure Is Inevitable

"Aunt Mallor I once was to you. Well, I go by Dr. Fitz these days. It's good to see you, Charlie." The woman brings her red curls over her shoulder, eyeing me up and down like a rotten piece of meat.

Already this feeling is mutual.

I haven't seen my mother's twin sister since her funeral. They look so much alike that it upsets my stomach. Accept my mom's hair was a lighter red and her eyes not so intimidating.

I don't bother crying out when guards detain me and Bucky. All I can do is stare at this person with an open mouth and shaky feelings clinging to my spine.

A few wet coughs fill the air. I guess there are sick people stuck in the group in the center of the field as well. No matter what they were all going to die. Those who still have plenty of life in them will meet the same fate as the ones who never stood a chance. I'm trying to find the irony of them both meeting the same fate but I can't wrap my mind around it.

Mallor Fitz rolls her shoulders with a wicked smile on her face. "It's time that you know the real story behind all this mess."

I scoff. My eyes water from the sudden bubble of laughter that forces its way out of me. Tears fused with humor slip down my face. They stare at me with bored expressions. Bucky's concerned gaze only causes me to choke up more profusely.

"Please, spare me your pitiful villain speech. It's ain't nothing I haven't heard before, doofus." The insult pours out of me before I can even think about what I'm saying.

She presses her lips together, forming a thin line. The wrinkles circling her eyes deepen as a sinister grin breaks onto her face.

I'm guessing she doesn't appreciate how funny I find this odd situation.

"I am the founder of the Facility Underground. A very advanced lab where extremely talented scientists were recruited to find the cure for cancer. But I wasn't the only one who started it. Your mother was my partner in this, Charlie. We had the vision to test the limits of the human body, together. She was the one who designed the facility and chose where it should be. Have you ever wondered who lives on the road behind your house? That's where the Facility Underground resides. God, you're more of a fool than your fucking mother." Dr. Fitz chuckles darkly, aiming her piercing gaze my way.

Whatever giggles consumed me before quickly drain from my body. There is a brutal flush that coats my neck and face.

The road behind the house doesn't even have a name. No one has ventured down its dirt path for more than a decade. I had no idea. How would I?

She takes three steps forward, her face only a few inches from mine. I smell fresh mint on her chilly breath. My skin crawls, begging to peel off my muscles and tendons to escape her cruel stare.

"She was the creative one. Always loved to design things and was great at it too. I had once hoped she'd tell you the family business and one day bring you by. Too bad she couldn't get over her fear of being caught by the government." Dr. Fitz shrugs her shoulders most nonchalantly.

"What the fuck does that mean?" I huff. Sweat streams down my nose and drips down my chin. The summer heat is getting to me. I see them leak sweat as well. Good. It's best to keep the enemies hot under pressure.

Her grin says a lot and yet utters nothing at all. I hate this woman already.

"Your mother began to grow paranoid about us getting in trouble with the real CDC. You see, it was our mission to go above and beyond ethical experimentation to roughly find the solution to the world's cancer problem. Meaning I gave most of our doctors a thumbs up for splicing human and animal DNA. Anything they thought necessary was good enough for me. But it was her, my sister, who didn't have a backbone.

178

After hearing her sweet concerns I knew something had to be done." She lets a confusing frown settle on her face. It causes her eyes to darken. A gloom encases her and I'm terrified to know why.

My heart beats like a war drum in my chest. Ugly anticipation thrashes inside my stomach, refusing to calm for even a second.

"She was going to blab about our work and I did what needed to be done to stop her. I only wish she went more quietly." I can't believe she's crying. Her tears are nothing compared to the ones I shed for my mom. How dare she?

I sniff harshly, slightly inhaling all the gooey snot that threatened to slip onto my lips. "Okay, maybe my mom was a part of some crazy mad scientist group, but she still must have had good enough sense to try stopping you." My defense is weak and we both know it.

"I started slipping her poison through our morning coffee. It didn't take long for her to start losing her fucking marbles and eventually become an alcoholic. You'd be amazed at the shit we've created at the lab. However, I had assumed she would die of a heart attack. Killing herself was... unexpected, honest." Ah, that's why her tears are falling still.

She loved her sister. My mother might have been the only person she ever cared for. And yet doing that had solidified who she was always meant to be.

"You're a monster." I let spit gurgle in my throat before shooting it at her face. The massive loogie lands in her slightly open mouth.

Her gag is music to my sore eardrums. She doubles over in coughing fits. The gruff squeals she makes influence me to squirm in the guard's hold.

Dr. Fitz wipes her face clean with the sleeve of her white lab coat and snarls at me. "Get a fucking grip. She's dead and there is nothing you can do about it."

Rage floods in my chest like a roaring fire. Flames beg to flicker from my palms. My fingers urge to curl and be tossed into her barely curved nose. Yeah, hearing the crack of it fill the air does sound good.

I don't realize I actually hit her until I'm tackled to the ground. My face hits the ground hard causing me to accidentally bite down on the inside of my cheek. Fresh blood seeps into my mouth. I spit again at her fancy white pair of heels. Who wears heels to a football field anyway? Oh, I know, fucking loser scientists who went too far.

"Damnit, Charlie." Bucky hisses at me and tries to rip away from his guards.

Dr. Fitz turns her attention to him, a gentle smirk playing on her lips. She tosses her hair again and flutters her lashes at him.

"Touch a single curly hair of his and I'll gut you!" My shout is muffled as the man holding me shoves my face into the grass. I unwillingly inhale dirt crumbs and choke on the green strands that find their way into my open mouth.

My estranged aunt crosses her arms over her surprisingly large chest and smiles at Bucky. Unfortunately, that is another thing we have in common.

"Your father has been the head of my security for a few years now. I guess I see why he wanted you to leave town for college so badly. You see, unlike him, I strive for all my last living relatives to want to be a part of my success. He doesn't wish that for you because he is a coward and doesn't deserve to even get to witness what goes on in my lab." She turns to look at his father.

A sad expression on her face but I know she is really disappointed. From what I remember my mom had one just like it when Dad tried hiding the liqueur.

"Dad?" He calls out to him. His voice cracks. The sound does its best to break me. I can't let it.

I can barely see his father nod his head in defeat and self-hatred. "At first, I figured it was a good-paying job. I never did think about the consequences. I'm sorry, Buck. No matter what, I'll always love you, son. I hope you find happiness in everything that you do."

That sounds off. My head is pounding and his words seem like a goodbye. Oh, shit.

Before I can even attempt to lift my head a little higher off the ground Dr. Fitz reveals a gun from the holster on her thigh and aims it right at his father's chest.

"Dad!" Bucky shouts as I cry out, "No!"

Neither of us can do a damn thing but watch my aunt shoot his dad like it's just any other day for her. I don't want to know how many people she's personally killed before this. The shot rings in my ears. The thud of his freshly dead father shakes the ground I lay upon.

She blows smoke from the gun's barrel. With one look from her, the guards remove our newly acquired weapons and toss them far away from us, making my machete thack onto the chain fence.

"Don't worry. I'll let you live. All you have to do is keep quiet and find your own way out of this town. Good luck, Charlie. Let's make this our little secret." Dr. Fitz gives Dr. Avery a glare which gets the woman moving with the guards now at her side.

Despite being free of their grasp I still linger on the grass, clutching it with all my might. One last guard takes a box of matches from his pocket.

"What are you doing with those? Hey, answer me." Bucky's voice trembles.

The guard smiles, revealing odd white teeth, and strikes a match. He tosses it onto the nearest prisoner and suddenly they're all on fire.

Screams and cries sing into the air. The smell of burning flesh fills my nose to the brim. I don't bother stopping the puke that shoots from my stomach and out of my mouth. I get on my knees and barf stomach acid. It stings my mouth and makes my eyes water all over again.

This is insane. All these people writhe under the blazing flames. There is nothing I can do to save them. We were too late. No, I was distracted by someone who was never family. Mother fucker!

Soft sobs make their way out of me. My breath hitches when a hand gently grips my shoulder. With my head shaking, I turn and tilt to peer at who I first believe to be Bucky. Instead, I find Dr. Fitz frowning down at me. This causes me to cringe and curl into myself. I look around and spot Bucky now unconscious.

On instinct, I try reaching for him. She stops me by yanking my shoulder back with all her might. I topple over and land on my back hard. The breath in my lungs flushes out. My vision is slightly impaired but I can still make out her as she stands next to me.

"I loved my sister. I want you to know that I wasn't always like this, a monster." I'm not given the chance to reach for her ankle when something I don't see coming whacks me on my forehead.

I wish that this sudden darkness will be forever. I don't want to wake up in this tragic world again.

22. Don't Go

Crust crumbles from my eyes as I flick them open. My head aches but the sight of the twinkling lights in the navy sky eases the pain. They shine bright against the dark blue canvas. A few clouds dot around them, hoping to block their bright beauty.

I feel dried blood on the side of my face. I bring shaky fingers up to touch the tender flesh of my cheek. A hiss flees my mouth as my hand grazes a fresh cut. I'll never properly heal if I keep getting slammed around.

"Shit." My shoulder pops as I scrunch into a sitting position. I should go find that douche who pinned me to the ground at the football field and give him a piece of my mind. Hell, maybe I'll shove his fat face into the ground and make him choke on dirt that tastes like earthworms. Yeah, I like that idea a lot.

But low moans filled with discomfort shake those violent thoughts out of my head.

I turn to my left only to see the small flower patch that used to rest in front of the bank. It's long been trampled to bits. Dead petals of red roses and broken stems of tulips are scattered about. Deep prints have been left in the still-drying mud from those who did their best to escape. Now they're cooling into crispy pieces on the football field. I knew people could be cruel, but that was otherworldly. My own family did such a heinous act. I feel sick just letting the scene flash into my head in all different directions.

Shaking my shoulders to rid myself of the terrible truth I shift on the chilly pavement. It's easy to ignore the loose pieces of the road that sink into my cut hands.

Faint clanking noises are coming from down the street. The Facility Underground is packing up their shit and getting out of this town. I doubt they'll tear down the fence. Elora Falls will be lucky if we aren't bombed off the map by morning when the real CDC catches wind of this.

To my right... Oh, they almost dumped us onto the block-buster doorstep. Its shattered windows greet me like solemn eyes who have lost their soul to horrible monsters. I can't say I blame the sight.

However, it is the boy my age sitting in a crouched position that causes my blood to simmer down into ice. Shards of it push through my veins. I ignore the icky twist in my belly and get on my knees, hands suddenly outstretched before me, seeking Bucky's bare trembling shoulders.

His letterman has long been tossed to the side. I don't remember him leaving the hiking and hunting store with it. I'm so tired I must be forgetting little things.

It's in soiled ribbons. I have no idea where his shirt is. His wonderful curls are limp with sweat from the sickness, they cling to his clammy skin that shines imperfectly.

As my jittery fingers grasp his shoulder. He jerks forward violently. I gasp when he topples over and lands on his side facing me. My mouth drops open in shock. To hide my sudden expression I cover half my face with my badly bruised hands.

"B-Bucky? We have to go now. C'mon before they really kill us." I force a slight chuckle.

He's still for a moment. Then his hazy green eyes stare at me with complete defeat and fear. My stomach leaps into my throat, begging to be released onto the pavement underneath us. I'm certain I have nothing left to puke.

Very precisely, Bucky shakes his head no and my heart snaps. "I'm so sorry. Please, forgive me."

A strange thumping starts at the front of my skull. It builds till tears drip down my face. Did I hear him right? No. He can't give up. Not yet.

"No, you gotta get up. We can find Dr. Avery or my aunt. They must have a cure for the Mush. They must!" Even I know I don't sound convincing.

He clenches his eyes tight. A dribble of pale green slips from his nose and down the side of his ashen face. Bucky wraps his arms around himself in an almost soothing motion. His large

186

muscular body curls into a frail fetal position.

"It's over for me, Char. We both know it. I've got maybe an hour left at this rate. But you have a chance to get out of here. Why be a stupid asshole and waste that chance to stay behind with someone w-who is fucking dying?" Bucky coughs roughly towards the end, vomiting thick green onto the street. It's getting into his hair and I have to force myself not to pull it back for him.

I shake my head in answer. I can't just leave him here like this. Oh, the pain he must feel from this. I only want to take it for myself so he can get out of town.

His hackle of disapproval for my obvious wishes to stay shakes me to my very core. I sniff harshly, inhaling the snot that attempts to escape my nose.

Silence follows. It takes its sticky fingers and grips me tight. I struggle to find words for him. He keeps his eyes shut. His breathing is becoming quicker and more shallow. Bucky is going to be falling apart soon. It may be mere minutes before the flesh peels from his disintegrating bones and forms an ugly pile of dark green Mush.

"I always thought you were the coolest chick around, you know?" Bucky's croaking words ruffle me out of this funk.

I rub my arms to get rid of this sudden chill that takes over me. I really wish I still had my favorite red raincoat. "Yeah, whatever you say."

His faint smile breaks my heart a little more. "You might have never noticed when I looked your way in the halls or searched for you in the stands at my games. I was always trying to find you. I hate that I made you and Shocker Pictures seem beneath me just 'cause I was this hot-ass jock."

Now that gets me to roll my eyes. A smile threatens to prick

187

at my lips but I don't have it in me to let it loose.

"It's funny because I always glanced at you in the halls too. But you were too busy having secret hookups with other football players and letting blonde sluts hang onto your shoulders. Don't worry about it. I forgive you." I fail to laugh at my own words. I meant for them to sound funny. I think it just came out rude.

His once lighter expression sinks into one of pain. He twists and shoves his face into the pavement and groans deeply. I see his flesh wiggle, begging to release from his perfect muscles and tendons.

I gulp down the bile that pushes into the back of my throat. Never did I know I had a weak stomach until people started getting sick in this town. "I love you, Bucky."

A half smile breaks through on his cracked lips. He looks so pale. All the luscious brown pigments in his skin hurriedly draining away as he attempts to get onto his elbows.

"I love you too, Char." He stays the words in spurts as he coughs and vomits.

I can't say anything more. Forcing myself to back away my backside hits the curb. In utter silence I watch this wickedness unfold before me.

Bucky violently convulses. His eyes roll in the back of his head. It's a matter of seconds and he is no longer the boy I love. He won't get the chance to grow up. And somehow I know I'm responsible for this.

My quiet tears have now morphed into terrible sobs. My chest cries out at me as I wail. My heart tears apart in a thousand ways. I've lost it all. There is nothing left of my friends or the people of this town. Why didn't I go with them?

Those glowing mushrooms begin to grow from what remains of him. I'm not sure why the sight of the swaying fungi gets me to talk.

"I remember the last game where you guys lost right before the playoffs. Despite losing, all the players danced their hearts out to the school song. We did too in the stands. It was us locking eyes that solidified my feelings and care for you. You searched for me like I did you. Yes, the rumors of your various situations did throw me for a loop but at the end of the day I was going to do anything and everything for you. Not because you were this awesome person that everyone loved, but because you were that rad dude who saw me for me and not some loser freak who likes telling people what to do in front of a dingy film camera. I will make sure the world knows your name and how you contributed to saving the people of Elora Falls." I snort.

I am the last person of Elora Falls left alive. I'm not sure for how long.

The dark sky is cloudless and shows off the stars. A pretty sight meant to be saved for the most special occasions.

"I think I'll always remember that sparkle in your eyes. Your bright smile will haunt my dreams and I'll let it." I like to think he can still hear me and that he's with the rest of our best friends in whatever fucking place greeted them after death.

By the time I finish spilling all of this, the mushrooms have grown to a disturbing height. My eyes have dried and I feel horrific. My stomach aches as odd bubbles of laughter travel up my throat and shoot out of my aching mouth. The glow from the fungi illuminates what's left of the Blockbuster windows. I see my dismantled reflection somewhat.

I'm a wreck and more pissed than I ever thought possible.

23. You're Going Down

I 've been sitting in front of this pile for a while now. Maybe a few hours at the most.

The lump of Mush has slowly been trudging down the street. It's moved a few feet and still has a long way to go. It must have the sense to join the massive mound in the forest just beyond my home. Well, my house. It won't ever feel like home and neither does this town. It's empty of the asshole people and bare of all the little quirks that made it bearable.

There is no camera or any kept footage of what we've seen. Nothing to pin this on Dr. Avery and Dr. Fitz. They will get away with this and there is nothing I can do about it.

All I feel like doing is continue to sit in silence and wait for the Mush to take me too. However, I don't feel any chills nor is my nose itching to sneeze. My insides wallow within me, not being torn apart by the evil science fungi.

It's a cruel joke. This thing took my friends and my dad. In all honesty, the Mush's first victim was my own mother. I am utterly alone in this fucked up place. Maybe I should lie here and die of starvation or thirst. At least it'd be on my own terms. And yet the thought causes my stomach to twist into knots.

I can't give up. I should go back to April Square and fight until I'm shot down or taken over by the Mush. Yeah, that sounds like a good idea to me.

Wiping the stale tears off my face, I stagger to my feet. My knees ache from sitting criss-crossed on the uneven street for too long. The off-white bones in my spine pop as I raise my arms high into the night sky.

I was so deep in thought that the Mush pile had gotten further than I thought it could. A break in the fence that surrounds the bank was found. I watch it slowly slither through, twigs snapping and leaves crackling underneath it. It's not long before I can no longer see its gruesome green glow.

Oddly, sadness consumes my chest cavity, flushing out any anger that usually settles inside me. All evidence of Shocker Pictures is gone. The funny thing about it is that none of us ever had any pictures together. I hate the irony in that.

With a shake of my head, I turn to face the suddenly

nonexistent wind. The noise continues from April Square. They must be compiling the last of their supplies. I have little time left before they leave me here on my own.

I should be glad that they are leaving. And yet there is a little ticking within me, telling me that this can't be over yet.

My skin aches with something on the lines of anticipation. It's being joined with a familiar feeling I get when watching the most grotesque of horror movies. This may not be a movie that I'm living in, but it sure does follow the most basic storyline. I need to play it out just right. Or else I'll be dead before I can get a few punches in.

I inhale a waft of summer air before stalking down back to the hunting and hiking supply store. Did they really think taking all my weapons was going to stop me? These idiots have another thing coming for them.

My ragged hair crusted with blood and Mush whips down my back with each step forward I take. I'm lucky I found a generic black hair tie wrapped around my wrist. The other one in my hair snapped when I was pinned on the field. I take my hair and tie it as tight as the band will go. My bangs settle awkwardly on my bruised and cut forehead.

Determination mixed with anger fills my blood, heating my heart. This is the perfect fuel. I feel like a monster truck on steroids right about now.

I know exactly what I need to grab when strutting into this abandoned store for a second time. My face is set in a calm expression despite all the crazed emotions that are running through me.

I find the case with many small knives and stuff a few into my pant pockets. I don't bother with another machete. But I retrieve another gun and more bullets. I want their deaths to be quick. There won't be time to welcome any torture, unfortunately. Truly, I don't want there to be a next time for that opportunity to present itself.

I wonder if they think I'm dead. Perhaps they don't care. Well, Dr. Fitz sure doesn't give two shits.

My steps are harsh and loud as I strut out of the store. I thump towards my newest goal, trailing down the street with ultimate purpose. They will see me coming. I will be the last thing they see before the light in their eyes goes out.

24. Going Down Hardcore

I n one of the large dark green bushes that surround most of the April Square border, I hide in plain sight.

I wait and watch a few of the military vehicles roll out. Most consist of medical support and soldiers. Two armed men hang on the sides of the tanks with their rifles ready for action. I fear they are either on the lookout for me or movement from the Mush because I'm positive that the mound in the forest is twice its size. I've yet to spot any of the doctors I'm searching for. I'm not sure if that's a good sign or not.

Many more pass by and still no sign of them. With a huff, I jump out of the bush and land silently on my feet. I'm a stealthy cat on the way to cause mischief and they better be ready for me.

The gun sits in my hand nicely and my fingers curl around the handle and trigger perfectly. Extra bullets jiggle around in my pants pocket as well. The chilled silver of the various knives I took press against the camo fabric of the pockets, biting my skin and keeping me alert of their presence.

April Square is an absolute mess. Evidence of the Facility Underground's chaos is everywhere. Most of the crisp white tents are still here, all of them limp and missing their poles. I'm guessing they weren't important enough to take back. Perhaps due to possible contamination.

Many pink hazmat suits litter the dark cobblestone. They're stark blotches to the once simple town. Seeing all of the various papers and face masks drift in the casual warm wind causes my anger to grow hotter. Were they just going to leave the place in absolute shambles? I can't wait till I get my hands on them.

I continue treading through the Square. My eyes are wide open, waiting to catch anything worth my time.

It's moments like these in epic films that just seem right. The hero looking for any stragglers or hidden villains that they can handle. This is my moment not only to see the destroyed Elora Falls truly but also to gather my rage and aim it at those who ruined everything.

Children either died of the Mush or were burned on the football field. They won't live out their lives and neither will my friends. The elderly who no longer walk the earth won't get a chance to tell their grandchildren all the wondrous tales of their lives. None of this has been fair and that fucking hits me hard in the chest.

There's a sudden itch on the back of my shoulder. After looking both ways in between two tents I duck down low to scratch it away. Once I'm satisfied that it's gone to the now burning sensation left behind by my nails I creep back onto my feet, straightening out my knees.

Voices cut through my red-tinted haze. I fall to my knees once more and rush behind the nearest lopsided tent. My heart pounds as I watch two visibly shaken nurses in ugly green scrubs hurry forth.

"All of this bullshit is insane." One of them says. She's close to my age with crisp blonde hair that's braided down her back. She wobbles after each step she takes.

"Don't worry. Once they destroy the town records we can all go to the Facility in Mountain. That way we can start over and act like this never happened." The other smirks to himself. The lamppost lights make his black hair look greasy and his dark eyes beady.

I fight the urge to scoff. Of course, they have backup labs. This was just a kink in their research. I shouldn't be surprised at all.

They both shake their heads and scurry away to one of the last two military tanks waiting at the end of the path. The second must be for the doctors.

Once they drive away I stand again and roll my shoulders back. If they're getting rid of everything about this town then I know exactly where they are. City Hall is just a few blocks north of April Square. Shouldn't take me long at all to get there.

My eyes and ears need to be ready to sneak up on them. I hold the gun low close to my upper thigh with both hands. I need absolute control over this thing. I'm not going to waste any bullets either so I must get them with one shot each.

It has to be done. I can't let them do this to other towns. Not for no fucking Russians or some sick government shit.

That bizarre citrus and rotting odor from the Mush in the forest curves throughout the town. I hold back a gag each time I inhale a breath. My lungs inflate with the stench. And yet I'm still perfectly fine. There is no sickness inside of me and that is alarming.

Vivid memories of Thomas peeling apart breaks across my mind. I jerk my head to get rid of them. But then flashes of Crista's pale green face take their place. I gasp as they seem to strike my heart with horrid blows.

It gets too much as the tears from Bucky's cloudy green eyes flicker behind my own. I accidentally toss my gun a few feet away from me and collapse to the ground. The grumpy payment tears the knees of my pants and scrapes my flesh.

Ignoring the fresh blood that attempts to pool around me I silently cry. My face dampens in a matter of moments. My chest aches and my throat seizes close.

This is the tragic part of the film where the hero realizes she lost everything she ever cared for. All because people wanted to be the best and prove that they own the world. I never wanted to be the hero. No. I'm meant to be behind the camera telling the actors what to say and how to say it. None of this should have happened.

And yet this is also the last turning point of any film with the presence of action or horror. The hero recognizes defeat and must summon all her will to fight back against evil and somehow make it out alive. I must do this.

I take a deep breath and force out the bad memories that try their best to pin me under guilt and sadness. Instead, I will let the happy ones to surface. Images of the movies with Shocker Pictures and football games with Bucky take over.

I'm grateful that I have enough feeling back in my body to get on my feet once more. I set a stern expression on my face to stalk forward. I pick up the gun with ease, settling it in my hands.

My feet move quickly, one foot in front of the other like it's nothing. The wind wipes my ponytail behind me. It grazes my arms and the skin of my shoulder due to the various slashes in the black material of the shirt. It's warm and somehow motivating. A bubbling emotion of either anger or determination keeps growing in my guts.

Before I knew it I marched to the front of City Hall. Its tall porcelain white frame glows in the darkness of the night. It seems that none of the stars shine on it, avoiding the place where more evil is being done. I don't blame them for it either.

The pitter-patter of my Converse hitting the stone steps echoes into the barren air. The noise wraps around my eardrums, clenching tight.

It's almost comical how movie villains expect the hero to walk right through the back door because they know they won't go through the front. However, I'm different and want these assholes to see me coming from a mile away. That sounds a little self-centered as I think about that. I rather not care at all. Any good morals I had died with my friends and my dad. I need them to shake in their boots and feel the fear that slithers through their bones and blood.

It's the only way I can truly dispose of them and rid the world of their wickedness.

The tall glass doors reflect my image. Fresh and old cuts litter my cheeks and forehead. My nose is still broken from the fight with Jake the other day. Damn, he's dead too.

My eyes are slightly swollen with purple and blue bruises. I look like utter hell. A bat out of Hell is more like it.

I'm surprised the doors are unlocked. I peel the right one open with all my might. Glass shouldn't be this fucking heavy. With a raging grunt, I manage to get the fucker open. A waft of nice cool air hits me. I practically welcome it with open arms as I carefully step inside.

The wide lobby is bare of people and proper light. The front desk is in disarray. They must have raided that first before getting to the back room where all the import papers are kept.

Most of the trash cans have been tossed to the floor, letting the garbage flutter around in piles of gross mess. It makes the place all the more terrible and its new renovations useless.

199

Damn, can't these docs get a real life and better hobbies?

A scuttling motion towards the back room catches my attention. I flip the safety of the gun and aim it before me. The newly polished hinges don't squeal as I gently push the swinging door open. Intense heat greats me head-on. An instant sweat breaks across my face and I'm already missing the perfect air conditioning in the front.

The many rows of file cabinets are ignited with a bright red light coming from a huge fire in the middle of the room. Four people surround it, their sinister cackles unsettle me.

I duck behind the closest row and watch them silently for a moment. Not only can I see them perfectly but also their green-tinted sweat that drips down the sides of their wrinkled faces. I guess payback does come around in various ways.

I came here to finish them. Not to watch a sickly Dr. Avery and Dr. Benson dump stacks of paper into the blazing fire on my aunt's order.

With grand purpose, I stand tall and walk out from behind the file cabinets with a grin on my face. My gun is raised directly at Dr. Fitz's back. How doesn't she feel my heated eyes on her? Hmm. I guess I'll have to get her attention in another way.

I straighten my shoulders and tilt my head a little. "I knew you pricks were jerks, but I never thought you would be cowards too."

Now that gets my estranged aunt to turn around and face me. Satisfaction bursts through me at the sight of her nose running a disgusting green sludge.

25. Not Today, Motherfucker!

The two of them behind her also slowly turn to see the newcomer. I give them all a wicked grin, hoping that it unnerves them.

Dr. Fitz sniffs harshly. "Finish up. We've got places to be. People to see. You understand?"

They listen to her words precisely. Out of the corner of my eye, I watch Dr. Benson collapse to the floor, her body convulsing. She's on the verge of falling apart just like her operation. Maybe she isn't too far gone yet to torment with her consequences.

"Y'know, Bucky went out the same way. He cried in pain and I couldn't do anything to stop it. All he was able to do was tell me how sorry he was before he shriveled into an ugly pile of green shit. When you die I hope you go straight to Hell and burn!" I shout to her in a sudden fit of anger. Did she ever care about human life? Most likely not.

Within seconds she's no longer a woman. Those irritating mushrooms sprout from her clumpy remains and illuminate the floor. I can't say that I'm happy to see one of the bad guys die like this. No matter how evil you are, no one deserves a death such as that. Well, maybe Dr. Fitz does. I'd love to see that happen next.

Speaking of my aunt, she twists around sluggishly to peer at the dead head of her Facility Underground. She mumbles under her breath but I can't catch what she says.

"Your mother was a fool for thinking we could actually cure cancer. I never had the intention of doing so. I just needed her smart mind to help further my research. And for your information, there were no Russians who tried to get a deadly viral weapon from Dr. Benson. That's a cover-up for my experiment from getting loose before the U.S. government could buy it from me." My aunt's cracked lips spread wide, showing off her newly rotten teeth.

Dr. Avery whips her head around after dropping papers from her shaky hands into the alarmingly high fire.

"What the fuck did you say?" Her hoarse tone scratches my eardrums in the worst way. She sounds like sharp nails scraping the green chalkboards at school. My stomach shrivels into my chest.

"Oh, please. As if I ever would tell you shit. You work for me and don't get a say in anything. That's how the Facility Underground works, Avery." Dr. Fitz seethes at the woman with wilted black hair that's plastered to her face due to sweat.

Hmm, a little trouble in their supposed paradise. All I do is stand here with my gun aimed watching their own little squabble play out. At least I'm being entertained for free.

"F-Fuck you." Dr. Avery sputters over a rough fit of coughs. She spits a thick slimy loogie near my aunt's heels. I gulp down the bile that rises in the back of my throat.

Dr. Fitz smiles like a mischievous cat and she willingly turns her back on me. My brows furrow in realization. She doesn't think I have the hairy balls to shoot her. Well, she's wrong.

Without a single thought about it, my finger squeezes the trigger and a striking shot rings out into the room. At first, nothing happens. Then a sharp cry clears my muddied mind.

There in the back of her left thigh is a gaping hole where dark green blood leaks down her pants. I did shoot her. I didn't even miss.

She limps around to face me with a gruesome snarl. "You little bitch! You have no idea what's going on here. Hell, too bad Mommy isn't here to tell you all the evil shit she's done to 'cure' cancer like she wanted."

Her words are meant to wound me. Despite me not wanting them to, they do, deeply.

I tilt my head in a silent question. She knows what I'm asking. Dr. Fitz obliges me even though there's a fresh bullet resting in her decaying flesh.

"Have you been wondering why you haven't caught it yet? This Mush that you like to call it? I have the answer to that.

203

It's so simple. I figured a movie freak like you would have figured it out by now." She isn't making any sense. Jeez, she must have been keeping tabs on me to know that about me. What a psycho.

"Wow. Spitting out nonsense. It looks like you're next to turn into Mush." I huff.

She scoffs. She takes a few steps toward me. I aim the gun again and she stops. She is smart after all.

"You might not remember your early years but I do. My sister would bring you to the lab and let you play around while she worked. One night, you slipped and broke your fall on a glass case filled with those pesky toads. Long story short, you were dying, bleeding at the neck. She begged me to do something, save you at any cost. I did so without question. That's how you got that scar." She points to my neck, directly at the jagged flesh that is hiding behind my ear.

I never remember it being there. Always, I forget about it. I haven't wondered about how it came to be. I assumed it was from a skateboard accident the day I met Thomas. He had let me try out his and I vividly remember falling.

This makes no sense. I shake my head quickly in a motion of disbelief.

"Okay, fine. I cut myself at such a young age that I forgot about ever being in the Facility Underground. Get to the fucking point." I sneer at her, fed up with her stalling antics.

Her last remaining minion is close to clearing out the entire record room. I've got to kill Dr. Avery and my aunt before they go after me.

Her ugly chuckles rub me the wrong way. I want to hit her so hard in the face. My hands are shaking with anticipation. My need for revenge and justice is eating me alive inside. Maybe that's the Mush finally taking me too.

"My only request to save you from bleeding out was to use your blood. She happily said yes and I finally had the perfect human sample to create the disease of my dreams. You, dear niece, are immune to the Mush. Now how is that for a twist ending?" Dr. Fitz cackles. Hysteria coats her in an invisible wave.

I stagger back. My arms go limp at my sides. I don't bother catching the gun as I drop it onto the black-and-white tile floor. This can't be real. No, I refuse to believe it. That's not possible.

I must have said that last part out loud because now she's snickering at me. "This fucking Mush shouldn't be real either but here I am dying from it. Good thing I'm not the only doctor in the network who has the blueprint for it. Let's call them my insurance."

This. Fucking. Bitch! I'm going to kill her and enjoy the hell out of it.

Now that I know I won't succumb to this sickness I can truly cause some damage. I kick the gun far away, almost hiding it behind a few rows of the cabinets.

"What are you going to do? Punch me?" She raises her arms to shed off her stained lab coat.

Dr. Fitz reveals skin-tight leather pants and a black muscle shirt. Damn, she even kicks off her heels. And yet the oozing lesions on her exposed skin cancel out the badassness.

I lift my hands to tighten my hair. A smirk blossoms on my busted lips as well. "Yeah, I'm going to sock you in the jaw and get a few licks in on your fuggly curved nose."

She bares her nasty teeth and charges me. I do the same, my hands open wide to instantly grip her red hair. We collide like battering rams. I'm instantly gripping her squishy neck. I literally feel those fucking mushrooms wiggle underneath her flesh. She doesn't have long. So I must make this quick and painful.

I roughly stomp my shoe onto her bare foot. Her yelp is oddly satisfying. But I'm not smiling as she takes my hair and twists. Hard.

"Fuck." I hiss when she practically tosses me around. My side collides with the nearest filing cabinet. I collapse too close to the pile of Mush that was once poor Dr. Benson.

She thinks I've had enough. With fluttering eyes, Dr. Fitz backs away to smack the other doctor on the back of her head. Her whimpers only prove that she is the big dog now turned little puppy. I ain't going down like this. Not in a fucking dumpster fire like the ones out on the streets.

Before getting on my elbows to lift myself up a slight glint hits me in the eyes. I jerk from the brightness only to catch a better glimpse at the gun I shoved away. Within seconds I grab it tightly and shoot up to my feet once more.

I click the safety off for a final time. She hears the flick of it and slowly faces me.

"Your pathetic mother didn't have the guts to kill me before I killed her. Now, run along and be happy that you aren't dead." She shakes her head in a disproving manner. Too bad I don't much like to take orders from assholes who think they're better than everyone else. I won't be treated like dirt. Fuck this bitch and the Mush.

"You talk too damn much, Aunt Fitz." I'm not given the chance to shoot her again when the last remaining two grunt and fall to their knees.

The convulsions start and so do the profuse vomiting. Nasty

green sludge spills around. The cracking of bones fills my ears and so do their cries. I don't feel pity for their pain. I change my mind actually. They do deserve this end. It fits perfectly.

I give a slight snicker before stuffing the gun in a random pocket of my pants. The weight of it is comforting.

Shadows from the many glowing mushrooms dance across the walls that are covered in ugly pieces of art dedicated to the city. The fire alarm finally kicks in and the water sprinklers douse the place. However, it's not enough to stop the flames from licking and burning everything in sight.

Smoke clouds the rooms and I'm forced to flee. I don't wait around to watch the newly formed Mush struggle to find the mound in the forest.

My lungs falter as I limp towards the entrance. Tears slip down my face. I'm not sure if I'm sad or relieved. It's most likely both.

The entire building is quick to be engulfed by flames the moment I hop off the bottom stone step.

I back up to reach the middle of the street. There is no summer breeze to welcome me or surprise rain to ruin the man-made fire. There's just nothing. Absolute silence.

The sound of nothing wills me onward. I don't give the burning City Hall a second glance. My body aches from being beaten on several occasions. My will to live is fickle.

A stabbing pain sparks in my heels. I ignore it the second I realize I'm heading in the direction of my house. It's going to take a while to get there. I might as well reflect on recent events. The thought of that gets me giggling. And then I'm sobbing while trudging on.

26. Time To Leave This Shitshow

S moke rises from behind the forest that surrounds my house. I've barely made it to the front porch and already the town of Elora Falls is gone. Burned to a crisp. The damn Facility Underground has long been abandoned, useless. There is nothing left for me to do or find.

By the change in color of the sky, I know the sun will be rising in two hours. Wonderful shades of purple have begun to appear. They push away the dark blue. It's the signal of a new day.

So badly do I want to collapse onto the porch and sleep. But the fire will eventually reach this place and I rather not burn with it.

I can't bear to go inside and find the place empty of my dad and my darling Copper. They both deserved better.

The alarming stench of sour soil and rotten flesh consumes my senses. I'm more than afraid to venture into the woods. It's waiting, growing into a gruesome monster who perhaps never wanted to be. And yet I must do so. It's the only way I can get free and run for the hills.

With a limp in my step, I hurry to the back of the house where the shovel lies. It's the same one we used to bury the rest of Thomas with. I'm utterly speechless to find the freshly packed hole now clearly empty of anything. It must have crawled out and joined the rest.

I can't worry about that now. My arms protest as I lift the shovel, pinning it close to my chest.

I want to look back at the place I grew up. Where I had my first argument with my dad and where I got my first period. Now that was fucking hilarious. Me and my dad both thought I was dying. Turns out I was just fine. However, that's when we both started to think about my mother. Some things he wasn't sure how to handle but that was just fine too. We managed. I will forever be grateful to him.

I'll miss my gnarly room and my collection of rad movie posters. But they're all just things. The people who I will miss forever are gone and won't be coming back. There is no point in me lingering here.

Clenching the wood end of the shovel, I stalk forth into the gloomy woods. There's a slight breeze that brings in dense white fog. It swishes against me, coating me in this coolness that my body now craves. It's easy to make out various-sized white toads with glowing mushrooms on their backs that hop to and fro. At times I hadn't noticed them and now they're everywhere. No doubt to congregate near the mound and call it their home.

They stir clear of me as I drift further into the thick trees. All of the pine and cedar tower over me, their branches threaten to reach out and snatch me into oblivion.

Twigs snap around me. The wicked sounds shock me, causing me to jump in my bones. Goosebumps flare across my flesh. This does feel like I'm walking through a horror film set. I should be entertained by this knowing that's been my perfect dream. And yet this has quickly become a nightmare.

The truly awful smell becomes overwhelming. I'm forced to shut off my nostrils with a pinch of my sore fingers. Somehow it doesn't do any good. The smell still clings to the inside of my mouth.

It doesn't take long before I encounter the mound. Yes, I was right. Only that it's tripled in size. The mushrooms are twirled around each other. Most are larger than my entire being. Their unanimous lights cause the trees to sparkle.

The green Mush pulsates a strange rhythm. There's an interesting noise that echoes from it. It's almost like thunder from a wicked storm.

Its fungi move in unison like they're a hive mind and the Mush it grows from is its queen or sorts. It's hard to describe what I'm seeing.

That's a sign for me to get the fuck out of here. It takes me a while to walk around the mound entirely without letting it snag me. Green slime falls from various tree branches. Puddles of dark sludge litter the ground, staining the once-pretty leaves.

Fuck. This is a swamp.

Once I'm certain I won't be sucked into anything I quicken my steps forward. The fence is just up ahead. I know I'll reach it before the fire sets upon the forest.

I squint for a minute to spot the right place to dig. Once the fog somewhat dissipates I see the fence more clearly. It surely does wrap around our small island. At least those fuckers were precise.

I jog the rest of the way and accidentally collapse onto the chain fence when reaching it. For a moment I catch my breath and shut my eyes. The sounds of the forest are different. There are no caws from ravens or chirps from crickets. Only the noise of the Mush flowing and the croaks from those infected toads.

The thought of those little creatures has me opening my crusted eyes. Somehow, like magic, there is one of those toads sitting before me.

It sits upon a large gray boulder a few feet away that is covered in soft pale brown moss. Its beady green eyes pinned on me. The mushrooms on its back leak a transparent yellow slime. I recognize this toad. It's the one that gushed into Thomas's hands. Oh, fuck no.

"You little fucker." I hurriedly climb to my feet and rush over to swing down the shovel.

To my surprise, it hops off seconds before I can squish it. I spin around and can't seem to spot it. It ran away.

I mumble under my breath. "Coward." As if the thing can understand me.

211

Those quick movements of mine only tire me more. I can't stay here any longer. I smell the treeline on fire. Ash drifts into the air. The mound of Mush will be next and hopefully all the toads as well.

It takes my remaining strength to dig up dirt from around the bottom of the fence and under it. I toss the dark ground behind me and over my shoulder. I shove the shovel so hard into the ground that I snap it in two.

"Shit." I curse to myself. I refuse to shed any more tears of dread and despair. With quick consideration, I use my hands to continue. My nails rip apart. Blood fills the deepening hole. The iron smell luckily snuffs out the Mush's rotting stench.

After what feels like a thousand years I finally managed to grunt my way under the fence to the other side. I don't have the chance to catch myself before I'm tumbling down the slope that leads directly to the rapid river.

My knee catches on a sharp rock. It slices the already ruined skin. I'm whacked around and my forehead collides with a fallen log right on the bank of the river.

All I feel is the cold fresh water before my vision escapes me. This is the part of the film where the hero is killed off after failing to save the day. And maybe I'm okay with that.

27. Made It Out Alive...

Freezing water pelts against me as I lie limp on the river bank. My eyes refuse to open. I do not blame them. I don't want to see the chilled fire ash drift in the air.

I hear various snaps from falling trees. It never made past the river. I should be grateful that I wasn't burned in my sleep. However, survivor's guilt is eating me up inside and I wish it were the Mush instead.

After cold shakes continue to course through me I've had enough. With a jolt, I'm sitting upright. My eyes dart open and I can see all the destruction. There is truly nothing left besides ash and the massive fence. The trees are gone and so is the mound. Perhaps that's the only good thing to come out of this.

And yet I can't help but wonder if anyone infected had escaped. Or if the Mush lingered on any of the nurses or doctors who fled before the town went up in flames. That thought alone gets me back on my aching feet.

I did wake up on the opposite bank. It was pure luck. The only way in and out of Elora Falls is mere feet away from me. I can see the stone bridge and the sickly remains that were once Jake. His body is still in ripped pieces rotting away. The smell of it doesn't faze me. Nothing will after having to constantly inhale the sickness that took my friends away from me.

Knowing that I unwillingly played a part in its creation makes me sick. I double over, vomit cascading from my split lips and onto my cut and bruised hands. I'm surprised my bones aren't sticking out from my frail flesh at this point. Everything that my stomach clung to shoots out of me quickly. I gag until there truly is nothing left to puke.

I wipe my hands into the flowing river. The cold water soothes the pains that linger in my fingertips. A satisfied sigh echoes into the air.

I refuse to stay here any longer. This time I ignore Jake's torn body and climb my way to the bridge. My hand latches onto the jagged iron poles that stick out the sides that the mayor never would pay to fix. They guide me upward, letting me hoist myself high enough to flip over the side.

Roughly, I land on my back. The troubled breaths in my

lungs fling out of me. I'm gasping by the time I manage to lean against the stone wall.

With grand reluctance, I shuffle tall and face what used to be a small town with little flaws that could have been easily fixed. All that remains is that damn fence. Mounds of fresh ash litter the land. The perfect green grass and massive trees have been burned into nothing. There are no more buildings and it sure as hell isn't a City Hall.

Dr. Fitz got what she wanted alright. I am the last survivor of this place and her colleagues still plague our world. If they truly have their hands on the Mush like she said then there is no telling if they will ever release it. Either way, I can't let that happen. Not after all I've seen and been through.

A strange idea filters in my mind as I turn my back on this wasteland.

My feet carry on. I let my arms and hands sway at my sides with each step. A pinchy ache in my shoulder jolts every time I stagger forward.

A sense of motivation settles in me. Someone mentioned a Facility in Mountain. There are only so many mountains in the states. And I doubt she would ever establish a lab outside the country. She was too insane to let foreign hands onto her most prized possession. Which means I don't have to search too far.

But the search will be long and dangerous.

Can I really do this on my own? If all my best friends were here they wouldn't hesitate to do it with me. Gosh, I miss them more than ever now. I'll never forget the dimples on Crista's cheeks. Thomas's mischievous laugh will haunt my dreams. And Bucky... his vibrant soul will never let me rest easy at night. I'll never get rid of his wicked smile when my eyes close.

The love I feel for him still won't ever fade.

Yes, I will find these doctors and exterminate them like they did all of us. It's only fair. They'll get what's now owed to them.

I'm more than halfway down the main road that leads to the next town over when the sun in the sky starts to dip low behind the treeline. Shadows are cast around me, almost as if they are joining me on my new quest. I welcome their company.

I listen closely to the chirping birds and rustling of foxes and rabbits. The noise calms me. Telling me that I made it out alive and I should be just fine. And yet I know this will haunt me for the rest of my life. I won't be able to just forget it happened. I don't plan to either.

I'll find a way to expose their whole operation, uncover more of their twisted secrets, and destroy everything that threatens the human race.

This is no longer some silly movie idea or a game. This is real life and I can't believe it took so many deaths for me to see that.

The gurgling in my stomach shakes the deep thoughts out of my mind. My mouth is so dry. I wonder if there is a stream or small river close by. I've never been outside of Elora Falls before. I've got no idea where anything is.

I should have made my dad take me on his work trips.

As the dying sunlight dims more I notice a big green sign with the name of a town.

Welcome to Earthville!
Pop: 5, 483

"Shit." That's way bigger than Elora Falls ever was. The newly formed excitement in me urges me forward. My steps are quicker than before.

By the time the sun is fully set I'm sprinting as fast as I can. In my mind, I'm doing my best to outrun the light of the full moon. I'd stop and admire the brilliant blue but I've got to get off the road and find a place to say. Hopefully, then I can regroup and look at whatever options I can come up with.

After a few more hours of exhausted running, I finally see a break in the thick forest that consumes this state. They open wide to a massive arch built from solid concrete. This leads to cobblestone that surrounds many large buildings like a police station and a town hall.

A smile spreads across my face. I can get help. There must be something they can do. I stop in my tracks abruptly. However, my sudden glee is instantly taken away by the flash of lights in my aching eyes. It takes me by surprise and I trip over my own feet, collapsing onto my rugged knees with a sharp yelp.

"Hold your hands to where I can see them!" A rough voice full of anger calls out to me from a short distance.

I know this part. Always do what they say to not get shot. So, with a tremor in my arms, I lift them as high as I can. Crusted blood breaks away from my bruised skin, toppling onto the ground around my knees. It creates a circle, encasing me in something only I truly understand.

"Are you a resident of Elora Falls?" The voice shouts again.

I take a moment to think about what answer I should give. "Y-Yes."

"There isn't an Elora Falls anymore." I don't want to cry but the tears start flowing anyways.

"Do you know what happened there?" He asks me. This time he steps forward and despite the many flashlights aimed at me I somehow make out his bushy blonde mustache and red cheeks.

Words cling to the inside of my throat. Can these people be trusted? Or are they the cleanup crew for the Facility in Mountain? I won't know until they have me in their clutches.

Maybe there's a way for me to get out of this.

"N-No." A lie. A big fat ass lie. It's the only way for me to continue to survive.

He pauses for a moment and looks around at the others who walk a little closer to me. From the little gold star on his chest, he's the sheriff of this town. I bet ours was in on this little disease-making lab too.

They look puzzled, somewhat afraid of me and of what I might have seen. They don't need to know.

"Alright, cuff her and bring her to the station. I'll get a hold of the doc on call." His order is carried out swiftly.

Instinct takes over as two female cops rush over to pin me to the ground. My face is shoved up against the cobblestone and I freak. My legs thrash and I shout out in anger and fear.

The flesh on my cheek tears open again causing blood to pool around me. The iron smell of it is like a slap in the face. I've seen so much blood. So much destruction. I want it to stop. But it can't if I fail to get out of this mess and find the Facility in Mountain.

"It's gonna be okay. You're safe now." The woman cop to the left of me whispers harshly into my ear. Her tone tells me otherwise.

I won't let them think they've won. Never will they win.

With all that's left of my heart and soul, I thrash hard and fight them to the police station of Earthville. Not even their pointed guns strike fear in me. I've seen darkness they've never could fucking imagine.

I'm shoved into the back of a squad car. I rebound and accidentally collide with the fence-like separator. I let out a rage-filled hiss. Perhaps I'm too much to handle with their bare hands alone.

As they drive off I continue to look forward and not back at the still rising smoke that was once Elora Falls.

Damn, the air cooling system in this shit box is wicked. A shiver takes over my spine and I squirm under its sudden grasp on me. My eyes want to so badly slip close. I let them.

28. The Mush

They never did take me to the station. Instead, I was brought to their large hospital and immediately examined.

I clawed nurses and kicked at least three doctors before one of them got smart enough to sedate me. My arm is forming a bruise from where they pricked me with a giant ass needle. That's when I shared a foul curse word that should never come out of a woman's mouth.

However, my eyes slammed shut despite me not wanting to go to sleep. The sleep was dreamless. No nightmares came to bang on my door. I had been granted a moment of peace before my body willed awake.

I woke up an hour ago dressed in a pale green hospital gown. Much like the one I'm sure Crista died in.

They scrubbed my face clean of the stale blood and ugly green goop that always took the chance to land on me. When infected people went out with the Mush they particularly liked to bubble like an erupting volcano. It just got everywhere.

A doctor with wild brown hair and large blue eyes sits in the chair across from me in this large room with no windows and pale pink walls.

His lip is slightly crooked but not too badly. He almost looks handsome. Well, I'd think so if I weren't currently cuffed to the bed rails. The cops said I was a danger to myself and those around me. He has no idea what I'm capable of.

"You won't talk to the police. Maybe you will talk to me about what happened." His light tone is oddly soothing. I hate it. I hate this place and everything in it. That sterile smell is permanently stained in my nose.

I stare at him with a blank expression. He shakes his head and stuffs his calloused hands into the pocket of his white lab coat. His look gives me the chills. Without thinking I pull the many blankets around me tighter. Nothing helps keep the warmth of my body contained.

These people must really fancy the cold.

"No one here will harm you, honest." He even brings his hand over his chest, giving me his best heartwarming smile.

Without straining, I shoot him a juicy spit that lands right on

221

his shoes. His lips twitch upward in disgust. Now that helps thaw my irritated expression. It's best when the supposed good fellows show their true colors. I'm no idiot, not anymore at least. I won't allow myself to succumb to their antics again. Over my dead body because they will need to kill me before I expose them all.

The doctor bends down to wipe away my spit. He swallows back a gag. Well, the feeling is mutual.

His older eyes slide over to me. They offer soft silent words that I refuse to buy into. They will not see me falter, not ever. I now have a mission to make sure this doesn't happen again. Suppose I can just stay quiet a little longer then maybe they'll let me leave. No harm must come to them.

Hell, if I must I'll snatch the surgical scalpel off the tray across the room and slice his aged throat open with one swipe. I only hope he'll test me on it.

After standing straight he gives a nurse with slim blonde hair a curious look. I don't like that at all.

"If she doesn't talk by morning then inform the sheriff that it's up to him, yeah?" He sounds tired. I wonder what from. Surely not due to me.

She nods curtly and scampers off to I'm guessing check on the other patients of this hospital.

Before walking out of this large room the doctor turns toward me one final time. His knowing smirk is all it takes for me to frown. I know that face more than I'd like. I was right not to trust him or these people.

Oh, fuck. This town has no fucking idea that the Facility Underground has even stepped foot here. I'm so dead. I thought I could beat them. I was wrong to think they wouldn't find me before I could get to them.

I watch him carefully retrieve a bright neon yellow badge from the inside pocket of his coat. He's too far away for me to make out what it says but I do have a good guess.

His heavy sigh is not a pleasant sound. The nerves that dwell under my skin move in a thousand different directions. They can't form proper information waves to send to my brain. All I manage to do is let my jaw drop in disbelief.

Being an amateur movie director, I should have seen this coming. In most horror movies the villain is never truly dead or missing. They seem to jump out of the shadows when the hero is starting to settle into their new lives or recover from their nightmares.

I fear this is one of those times.

"I've been sent to exterminate the last survivor of Project Mush. You can take credit for their naming of it." After giving a fake yawn he stuffs his official Facility in Mountain badge away and moves to remove something from the back of his pants.

A quick burst of panic floods my guts. In a hurry, I rise in the medical bed and pull the blankets close to my chest as if to shield myself from the small crisp black gun that's being aimed directly at my suddenly sweaty forehead.

This assassin of sorts clicks the safety off and tilts his head. "It's nothing personal, Charlie Everett. It's what I get paid for. I'm sure you can understand."

"Yeah, whatever it takes to pay the bills." I give a nervous huff.

With the gun still pointing at me in one hand he removes his coat with the other and reveals very stealthy black pants and a tight long-sleeve shirt the color of dark coal. I'm not even sure how he gets his hair smoothed back so well. Damn, wouldn't that be an epic final scene of a movie?

"Any last words to send along to my boss?" His slightly casual and cliche question releases a gruesome darkness within me.

These aching spots on my arms and back seem to lessen as they suddenly split open. Lesions are oozing much like the ones I've seen on Crista and Thomas. The yucky stuff dampens my hospital gown. Something warm drips on my hands that are clutching the itchy white blanket. The sight of pale green with a slight glow causes me to grin.

I clear my throat. "I'm cold."

The trigger is squeezed and something sharp hits me in the face. I'm falling back onto the bed with a thud as the ringing in my ears starts. It's too late to struggle or yell out in shock.

I'm dead.

Gone.

But not by the Mush.

So that evil sickness can go fuck itself and the crazy aunt who made it too. I'll see them all in Hell if I'm lucky enough.

Epilogue

Destruction is a concept I was never meant to understand. I find myself mulling over what I've seen others do to their own kind simply for power and pleasure.

As I perch on the chilled cobblestone of this vacant bridge and watch the green-tinted smoke rise high in the sky I can't help but wonder about one thing that's been bothering me since the start.

Why did humans force evolution upon me when my species was never meant for it?

The certain laws of nature are in place for a reason. To keep nature in balance forever. But of course, humans decided they were the superior species and broke the rules, defiling the natural order of life and death.

They should have seen this beautifully played destruction coming. I know I did the moment I was let loose from the lab.

With each hop I took to further get away from that ghastly vent the more knowledge my brain gained. By the time I deeply ventured into the humid woods I could understand human language and determine all the colors. My eyes changed too, allowing me to properly make out shapes.

I know for a fact that it was by mistake. The scientist needed my blood and tissue for their experimentation. They didn't expect other things to occur.

A gentle dousing of rain steadily swoops in and wipes out the smoke that is the last remnants of the Mush. I heard that one young blonde human call it that. Careful patter of the thick drops echo on the bridge, creating a circle around me, locking me in a brilliant bubble.

There is a tinge of pain that lingers in my lumpy back due to the destruction of this magnificent disease that sprouted from me. It did its absolute best to thrive under these odd conditions. It should have been properly guided by their medical ways. Then it wouldn't have been so easily barbaric and wreak havoc in so little time.

The pustules on my back continue to leak their comforting slime. It coats my rough skin and creates a slightly chilled barrier on my body to keep moist and safe.

Sadness will forever be steeled around my little heart. I was utterly disappointed when my accidental creation fled into the world only to be burned to a crisp by the ones who wanted it.

I did my damn best to wield it in the right direction. It answered my calls. A connection I had with it. Now it's severed and I'll never feel the warmth of it linger in my body again.

There is nothing left of it here. All evidence is buried under soft gray ash. I must leave this place and venture somewhere where I may start again.

Yes.

I favor that idea quite a bit.

My bent legs move on their own. I carry myself away from this horrid aftermath and venture out into this new territory. As I drift down the road a white and blue truck the shape of a box trudges down towards the fence and now nonexistent town. I ignore it. It has nothing to do with me anymore.

The forest outside of Elora Falls is much more rich in damp and hiding places. This is the perfect place to start anew.

I hobble deeper into the thick trees. The massive canopy hides my moist body away from the blazing sun that sets high in the sky. I rather not think about the time of day. It's much too human I gather. I may be smarter than all the rest of the toads but I rather not be associated with the kind who wronged me over and over again.

After a while, the bright sunlight dims enough for the branches and leaves to cast their grand shadows on the forest floor. In this new sight, I manage to spot the perfect place to fester within.

A simple broken log with dark space and a perfectly round entrance hole is hidden beneath a strangely carved boulder. This is exactly what I've been searching for.

I hop inside and inhale the soured air that fills it. It grips my small lungs tight and I do my best to smile.

Once I thoroughly examine the hallow long I burrow myself into the pile of moss, leaves, and dirt that has been gathering within it. My lumpy being sinks into the mess wonderfully. I feel the glowing mushrooms on my back sway with glee. Yes, I know this will be a grand place to let my creation spark a better life.

That scientist still may yet possess all they need to create another like me. However, it will never be as great as mine. I shall smother it until it becomes too fantastic that the whole world will fear its beauty.

That sounds wonderful. Perhaps there is a purpose for me after all.

Something in me whispers. I need to let go and allow the roots to take hold. As if it understands my agreement, my body begins to slip away, falling into pieces. I ignore the sharp pains and upsetting breaks of my fragile bones.

The Mush does its natural ways and slithers around my mess. I can barely see it latch onto the walls of the log. Its glow is a mighty one. This is what I was meant for.

As I die I watch my creation bloom into a truly monstrous beast that is so beautiful that I cry ugly yellow tears. It's a shame that I cannot live long enough to observe it take over the world and all its torture and pain.

Humans will learn to appreciate this as much as I have. Now I may linger here and wait for the decay to commence.

Yes, I much like this death.

It suits me.

He was only gone for a few days. What happened?

Mr. Everett put the mail truck in park before leaning against the wheel with a gaping mouth.

Remnants of green smoke filter through the sky as he carefully gets out of the rusted vehicle.

The pale hair on his legs that is exposed by his khaki shorts stands straight in confusion as well as a little bit of fear. He is so sure he came down the right road.

Sometimes the state gets all twisted and he accidently travels down the wrong street to deliver packages. And yet he isn't sure this is the case.

However, the welcome sign of Elora Falls is right next to that strange fence that's around the border. That wasn't there when he left. Oh, there's a dead body near it.

Many thoughts run through his mind. He shoves his trembling hands through his fraying hair. Panic sets into his chest like a wicked rattlesnake.

If the town went up in flames it would have been in the news. He'd see a paper anywhere with it being the headline. And yet his usual out-of-town stops hadn't said a word. No one may know.

That can only mean...

Mr. Everett takes two steps forward and collapses to his knees in a fit of hysteria. He knows what this means. There could only be one reason why the town no longer is right in front of him. Damnit.

He should have listened to his wife all those years ago. Of course, he had been aware of what she really did. But it wasn't supposed to get bad. That's what she promised.

That sickness must have been the Facility Underground's fault. They wiped the whole town out. Including his daughter.

She must have been so scared and confused.

That realization only makes him sob harder. He should have been here. Instead, he chose to go on an emergency mail run for the mayor. And because of that he is forever alone without his dear child. Why must a parent outlive their kid? It was never meant to be that way.

His wails infiltrate the atmosphere. "Charlie! Charlie."

Charlie.

Charl.

Char....

The End.

Acknowledgments

I truly want to thank my bookish/author bestie Lily Gray who wrote the fabulous thriller novel *They Found Us*. This book would not have made it off the story outline if it wasn't for your awesome enthusiasm and complete interest in it. I utterly appreciate all your advice and honesty. You've helped so much in this process. Thank you.

I'd like to thank my family for their continuous support of my dreams and writing goals. Your faith in me will always mean very much to me. I would have never had the motivation to write my heart out if it wasn't for y'alls love and helpful words of wisdom.

And of course, for the people who have willingly stayed for the journey and showed interest in this book, thank you. It's amazing to know there are people out there who are more than willing to read what I've written. One day my small group of fans will get bigger. It will all be because of your much-needed support.

Again, thank you all so very much!

About the Author

Harlie has been a passionate writer for years. She enjoys fantasy romance and horror novels the most. Her favorite books of all time are The Hobbit and Interview With The Vampire. When she isn't writing, Harlie can be found rewatching her favorite TV shows and movies or spending time with friends and family. This is her debut novel in the horror genre and she hopes to one day be a full-time writer. She lives with her family and many pets.

Also by Harlie Hargraves

Harlie is also writing an ongoing adult fantasy romance series with book one and book two on the way!

Out Now!
Anna Scarrow had wanted to be a knight her entire life. Upon her father's sudden death she travels to Thrallen to illegally compete in the legendary Knight Trials. Not only does she have to fake her identity but Anna is also being hunted by the royal warlock for the possession of forbidden magic.

Coming Soon!
Besides barely surviving the Knight Trials and rising from the dead, Anna is thriving. However, being on the outs with Crowlen is never a fun feeling. Well, that's no matter when her brother King Kasper is set to marry the darling Sarafina. But nothing seems quite right due to an unexpected wedding guest who's determined to steal the show.